CHARLES THE THROWBACK

ted owen

LOST
COAST
PRESS

CHARLES THE THROWBACK
Copyright ©2006 by ted owen

Lost Coast Press
155 Cypress Street
Fort Bragg, CA 95437
(800) 773-7782
www.cypresshouse.com

Cover and book design: Michael Brechner

Publisher's Cataloging-in Publication Data

Owen, Ted.
   Charles the throwback / Ted Owen. -- 1st ed. --
Fort Bragg, CA :
Lost Coast Press, 2006.
     p. ; cm.
   ISBN: 1-882897-89-7
   ISBN-13: 978-1-882897-89-6
   1. Calves -- Colorado -- Fiction. 2. Beef cattle -
- Colorado --Fiction.
3. Cattle--Breeding -- Colorado--Fiction. 4.
Ranching--Colorado--
Fiction. 5. Ranch life--Colorado--Fiction. 6. European
bison--
Fiction. I. Title.
   PS3615.O946 C43 2006
   813.6 -- dc22 0511   2005906732

Printed in the United States

9 8 7 6 5 4 3 2 1

Acknowledgments

My now deceased Uncle Cecil was a newspaper reporter whom I worshipped as a youth. I sent the first two chapters of *Charles* for his perusal. He was undoubtedly well into his cups when he read them. His unkind remarks made me realize that Cecil, like Hemingway, had become a worthless drunk offering arrogant advice. I resumed writing and continued learning.

Also involved in the writing of *Charles* was David Harris, a retired professor of English with whom I became acquainted in a local poets' group, the "Root River Poets." David's tolerant review of both my prose and poetry encouraged me greatly.

I am indebted to both of them and to unnamed others.

His Birth

CHAPTER 1

Within the hour of his birth, Charles was observed by three individuals, each of whom felt a different emotion.

His mother, an old Hereford, perhaps sensing that this calf, her seventh issue, would be her last, felt more than her usual amount of love, and was so protective that she was not about to let the rancher handle her newborn.

Rancher Jim Radson, out for a walk before breakfast and wet to the knees with morning dew, looked at Charles and swore aloud, "Red, dammit! Red! Ye gods! A Hereford cow bred to an Angus bull is supposed to throw a black calf with a white face! What the hell happened?" Angrily, he threw the stick he was carrying at the old cow, who'd been standing him off from her calf, then stamped off toward home and breakfast.

The third individual to view Charles happened to be his Black Angus father. Had he happened by a few minutes later, Radson could have cursed him too. The bull showed nothing but complete indifference toward the calf. Black Hercules, Charles's sire, barely glanced at the cow and their new offspring, who lay some twenty yards from where he was busy stuffing himself with the new grass of June.

Winter on this Colorado high-country ranch had been very hard on Black Hercules, a former native of Nebraska. The long cold stretch had removed much of the fat that normally lay beneath his thick hide. Black Hercules was far more interested in filling his paunch than in his newborn calf. Black Hercules was, quite simply, not very bright! He was a product of too much line breeding (inbreeding if you prefer). He closely resembled those pictures printed in various farm publications by the Aberdeen Angus Association, and was therefore, in the eyes of rancher Radson, exactly what was needed to improve the CR herd. Long of body, with the wide rump typical of the Angus breed (imported into the United States in 1873 by a George Grant), Black Hercules was expected by Radson to improve the quality of his calf crop. Hercules had started out well enough by having impregnated his share of the CR cows the previous fall.

The bull's parents, should you care to call them such, were a curious combination of father-daughter and brother-sister matings that produced some odd-shaped offspring as well as the stylish Black Hercules. The practice of inbreeding accentuates weaknesses as well as desirable traits. A good breeder would cull—discard by marketing—all those inbred offspring possessing undesirable traits, and retain those with valuable qualities for further propagation. Most of Black Hercules's half brothers and sisters had been culled.

The Nebraska cattleman who had raised Hercules was, unfortunately, more a salesman than a herdsman. A truly good breeder of cattle would not sell a bull for breeding purposes until it had been proven; once his calves were born and shown to be of good quality, the bull would then be offered for sale. Naturally, this process cost extra time and money.

Well advertised, well groomed, but still unproved, and standing docile in the show ring at the Nebraska cattle auction, Black Hercules had appeared to rancher Radson the ideal Angus sire. Genetically, however, Hercules was a flop!

Drawn to the Nebraska auction by some glorious advertising, Radson—a new and therefore green rancher—successfully fought off all other bidders to trade more than top money for

Hercules. While returning to Colorado that night, the unsuspecting young man would not have been so proud had he known that the handsome black bull riding in the new trailer towed by his new pickup truck was in reality a big black bag of genetic tricks.

James Radson, who'd chosen Black Hercules as the perfect sire, was himself something of an oddity. Born and reared on an Iowa farm, he reached maturity during the Korean War, enlisted in the air force, and served four years as an aircraft mechanic. Upon returning home at the end of the war, he found no opportunities awaiting him. Iowa's greatest export during that period was its youth, so Jim Radson flowed along with the tide to Denver, Colorado, where he met his bride — also an Iowa expatriate — and took up the carpentry trade during the building boom of the sixties.

In Denver he'd struck up a friendship with an electrical contractor named John Colvin. Radson was a frank and open person; Colvin a rather devious sort. Throughout the '60s Colvin's contracting business flourished, while Radson, who'd always worked for others, merely acquired a bad back from all the heavy construction work.

Before supper one evening, over more than a few bottles of beer, the Colvin-Radson ranch was born. Radson, confessing a secret desire to be a rancher, and Colvin, looking for a tax loophole to hide some of the profits from his growing electrical firm, managed to miss their suppers, while they built their ranch to a size rivaling that of the famous King Ranch of Texas. They also created a king-sized mound of empty beer bottles on their table before heading home to their respective angry wives.

On the premise that where three should fail one would succeed, these two prospective cattle barons bought out and combined the ranches of three separate, and rather grateful, elderly ranchers who'd each labored a lifetime near Eagle, Colorado. Thirty years of hard work had almost cleared the old-timers' properties of debt. The high price that Colvin and Radson had promised for their holdings would allow them to spend the remainder of their lives in relative ease—if, that is, the CR Ranch should succeed. The three old fellows had opted for the highest price offered, and had sold contracts for deed. Titles were not exchanged, and only a portion of the money promised was given. Many hopes rode on the success of the newly conceived ranch.

The CR Ranch comprised approximately 3,000 acres and lay about ten miles south of the town of Eagle, which was high enough in the Rocky mountains—7,200 feet above sea level—that its residents spoke of the weather as consisting of eight months of winter and four of tough sledding. Of the 3,000 acres, 2,500 were steep mountainside covered with aspen, scrub pine, and sparse shade-grown grass on which only mule deer and elk could survive and on which cattle would almost starve. Only 350 acres of the CR were valley meadows; half of them were irrigated, and that half produced all the winter feed for the cow herd.

In addition to the owned land there were leases for nearly 20,000 acres of grazing rights on government-owned forestland. These rights were also nearly worthless, except for one thing: a bald mountaintop consisting of 1,200 acres that produced lush grass throughout the summer.

Colvin and Radson felt that they would enjoy greater success than the previous owners had by applying all the latest and most scientific practices to their operation. Radson had read in his various stockmen's journals that the crossbreeding of two pure-bred lines such as Hereford and Angus would produce offspring of greater vigor. The purchased herds of the CR were mainly of the Hereford breed, which explained the purchase of Black Hercules. Charles's mother appeared to be a Hereford cow (white face with a reddish-brown body.) Actually, she was just a plain old range cow: a hardy mixture of mostly Hereford, a little red poll and, way back in her ancestry, some Texas Longhorn. Had she been of purebred Hereford ancestry (as were the first Herefords brought to Kentucky by Henry Clay in 1817), Charles would have been born all black with a white face and without horns, or polled. Yet there he lay, wet and steaming on that cool early June morning, all red and worse to come: he would eventually grow horns. Genetically, he had only one chance in sixty-three to have been born red colored and with the genes that would allow him to develop horns.

Charles's color was what caused Radson such consternation on the morning of his birth. Charles's mother, sometimes called "Old Maude" by Radson's wife, was a bit too rangy for a Hereford, but she was reddish and had short, erect horns. Over a hundred years before, Maude had an ancestral dam who was once claimed by one Samuel Maverick.

Sam Maverick was a shrewd old Texas rancher of the late 1800s who refused to brand his cattle, thus being able to lay claim to any unbranded critter in the area. Maverick may have profited from his little scheme, but in the process he also picked up and added to his herd some of the wildest, most knot-headed, ornery long-horned cattle around. The local cowboys soon gave old Sam's last name to any wild-eyed animal that refused to herd properly.

Charles's mother was a maverick! Always on the edge of the herd, and ever ready to bolt for the nearest timber whenever the chance arose. Deep within her she carried one driving urge: that she and hers should survive.

Geneticists who breed cattle deal with numerous genes, and, though they do not care to admit it publicly, their science is a rather inexact one, whereas geneticists who breed seed corn like to tout their profession as an exact science. Nonetheless, out of millions and millions of highbred corn plants growing in a field, one now and then turns up with seeds on the tassel—like teosinte, an ancestor of maize, which we now refer to as corn—rather than in an ear attached to the stalk. The geneticists airily toss off these plants as "throwbacks."

Unknown to all those present in the meadow that morning, Charles was a throwback.

Mentioned in the Bible and in other early writings of man was an animal that once roamed the whole of Europe: the aurochs. Most historians believe it was the wild cattle known as aurochs from which man managed to domesticate and breed the cattle we now have. The now extinct aurochs had red hair, a massive head, broad shoulders, a narrow rump, and large, erect lyre-shaped horns. Aurochs roamed the wooded wilds of Europe until man invaded, destroyed the forests, and pushed the Aurochs into oblivion.

Charles, the throwback, the stalk of corn with the seed in the tassel, that red, wet lump lying in his mother's shadow, would grow to resemble his ancient ancestor, the aurochs!

CHAPTER 2

About three hours before Charles's birth, Loren Smith, or Smitty, as he was known to almost everyone — crawled out of bed and, once fortified with but a cup of coffee, stumbled off to work. May through July were the only months of the year when there was enough light to see while on his way there. During the other nine months, Smitty had already been swallowed up in the catacombs of the packing plant where he began his toil long before the sun rose.

Unlike rancher Jim Radson, Smitty didn't wake up at dawn unassisted. It took the incessant clamor of an alarm clock and his wife's foot in the middle of his back to get him up and moving. Perhaps the difference in the way these two woke to greet each new day was that every morning brought some new challenge along with the daily chores for Jim, while Smitty could only look forward to more of the same old crap. He knew exactly where he'd be and what he'd be doing every hour of each and every working day.

Smitty worked in the hog-cut department at a packing plant in a southern Minnesota town. Every weekday the workers of the "kill" department slaughtered five to seven thousand pigs and hung them on a continuous chain running into the plant's mammoth coolers. On the following day, promptly at six A.M. the chain started moving again, delivering eight carcasses per minute to two conveyer belts reaching into the hog-cut department. The

7

chain then returned to the kill department for another day's supply of freshly killed pigs.

Smitty's station and job lay approximately halfway down one of the hog-cut conveyers, where he sliced pork loins off the remainder of the carcass with a two-handled curved knife shaped something like a carpenter's drawknife. By the time the hog carcass had reached Smitty, it had been split down the spine, each half going down a separate conveyer. The hams, head, and shoulder cuts had already been removed.

At the age of twenty-eight Smitty had accumulated seven years' seniority and had progressed through four job grades. Grade five, his present level, was the top pay grade he would ever achieve at the plant. Unless he went after a foreman's job — highly unlikely due to his personality — more seniority would not net him any more pay, just a less physically demanding job. His starting job had been grade one, on the kill line, yanking entrails from the slit stomachs of fresh-killed hogs.

Smitty was often surprised to find himself driving off to work in the predawn gloom. He'd completed three years of college successfully, if somewhat indifferently, yet here he was back in his own hometown, going to work daily in the same plant where his father had labored for thirty years before his death. Looking back, Smitty had come to the conclusion that the cute little coed who'd become his wife had intrigued him more than his studies at the university. An unexpected pregnancy, the death of his father, and the loss of any financial support had driven him back home and into a dead-end job at the plant.

The fruits of his seven years' labor had produced a house with a thirty-year mortgage, a two-year-old car with thirty-three monthly payments remaining, two daughters now in school, and a wife now on the pill and with interests centered almost entirely on her daughters and her coffee-klatch friends.

As for hobbies or ambitions, Smitty had practically none. He read sporadically—mostly biographies—and hunted and fished a bit in season and on the weekends allowed by wife Barbara. Of relatives and personal friends, he had practically none, no brothers, no sisters, mother and father both dead, all other relatives living in remote places. Perhaps the closest friend he had was the fellow who worked across the table from him. Robert "Bob" Bine had been in the same high school class as Smitty and Barbara, but they had not been good friends at the time.

Another classmate who'd grown up next door to his wife also worked in the plant. His name was Theodore Berge, better known as "Teddy," even though he preferred Ted. Teddy, as he was derisively referred to throughout his miserable time in school, was a nerd: short, fat, and non-athletic, his myopia forced him to wear thick glasses. All of his classmates treated him like a nerd; consequently, he became one. No one liked him.

Teddy, who could not attract and was not found attractive by the girls, was often laughed at by the jocks who had the full attention of all of the girls. Smitty, strangely enough, sensed the cruelty in everyone's behavior; he refused to participate, even though he too considered Teddy a nerd.

Upon graduation from high school, Bob Bine enlisted in the army, while Smitty and Teddy went off to college. Smitty never finished. Teddy acquired a degree in history, which he came to realize was next to worthless in the real world. In something less than three years, Bob and Smitty found themselves laboring away back in the plant. Teddy, who could find nothing else, wound up as an accountant in the same plant's payroll department two years later. On the rarest of occasions, two to three times a year, Smitty asked him to join Bob and himself for a beer or two after work, for which Teddy was extremely grateful. Teddy had no friends at all.

All in all, one might say that Smitty's life was not a happy one. For simply trying to "do the right thing," he found himself fenced in by the rest of the world.

Work on the hog cut became so tedious that it sometimes was dangerous. Razor-sharp knives and the constant mind-numbing motion of the dissected carcasses on the line had caused so many bloody accidents in the past that the union had insisted on a ten-minute break for every sixty-five minutes' work. The continuous motion before their eyes actually caused some workers to stagger like drunks when the line ceased moving for the break, in much the same manner that sailors sometimes would stagger down the gangplank on wobbly sea legs.

Plant management employed safety engineers, but there were still enough accidents occurring for them to retain a full-time doctor. Two or three times a day the company doctor had a chance to practice his skills with needle and suture on some hapless soul—a neat scar on Smitty's left hand bore witness to his artistry.

For the sixty-five-minute work period between breaks, Smitty and three of his coworkers were required to stand in the same place while slashing loins from the remainders of the carcasses flowing by. Slash, flop, push-one; slash, flop, push-two; and so on up toward 400 before the infernal belt stopped its progress for the long-awaited ten-minute break. The time was supposed to be used for sharpening knives and policing the area, etc., but most of the workers managed to sneak off to the latrine for a smoke. Smitty always went along to with them, even though he'd given up tobacco several years before. He went just to get away from the damned conveyer. Furthermore, it was warmer in the latrine, for the federal food inspectors required that the temperature out on the floor be kept below fifty degrees Fahrenheit to retard the growth of bacteria on the meat.

On this particular morning, Smitty, as usual, met his counterpart, Bob Bine, who pulled loins across from him on the other line. Bine was a garrulous extrovert; Smitty much more introverted.

"Hey, Smitty? How's it goin?" was Bine's standard greeting, in reply to which the taciturn Smitty could just manage a grin.

"You remember I told you about my cousin who's married to that rancher out in Colorado? Well, I wrote to her and also to the Colorado Department of Fish and Game about elk hunting. How about it? Made up your mind to go? Elk season is early this year, so the weather should be good."

After a bit of thought, Smitty replied, "Yeah, why not? I'm so damned sick of this grind I'd better go."

Thus was made the decision that would bring Smitty and Charles together for the first time one October afternoon high on a Colorado mountainside.

CHAPTER 3

The bald-topped mountain that rose behind the newborn Charles would soon become his home. That mountain, since the very beginning of its existence, had always been host to some sort of life. High up on the mountainside, a small herd of elk had been gradually working their way higher and higher, following the receding snow line upward. Cow elk would leave the herd for a couple of days, give birth, and then rejoin the herd as soon as their calves were able to travel.

While winter may have been hard on Black Hercules, it had been even harder on the elk. Eight cows, four calves, and three yearlings belonging to a huge old bull elk were pushed down the mountain by the snows of the 1974–75 winter, and made their way to their winter pasture. Once there they found the CR Ranch's cattle firmly entrenched on the elks' historical winter food supply.

Jim Radson and his two sons had cut the hay from practically all of the valley land, and had it stored behind twelve-foot-high fences that would keep the hay safe from all the elk and mule deer of the area, for both will climb to the tops of haystacks and urinate, and cattle will not eat hay thus contaminated. This hay was the meager fare that had pulled the CR herd through the winter in reasonable condition—all save Black Hercules, who needed Nebraska corn to keep all his fat in place.

For centuries, elk had descended the mountains every fall to graze the valleys around Eagle, Colorado, throughout the cold

12

months. The winter beginning in '74 had truly been hard on the elk. The cows, calves, and yearlings belonging to the old herd bull—Harold as he'd been dubbed by Radson's wife—had been joined first by one and then two other young bulls in December, bringing the herd total up to nineteen.

Once the rutting season had passed, Harold found he could tolerate the two young bulls back in the herd again. During the winter, poachers had killed one of the young bulls and two cows, and two more cows and two calves had died of starvation. The survivors managed the winter by eating whatever they could find: a little hay left standing along the creek bank and the edges of the fields, plus twigs and bark gnawed from aspen trees. Toward the end of January they were so hungry that they would even mingle with the CR cattle to snatch a bit of the hay spread by Jim and his sons. Normally very shy, they would have stayed in the woods by day and foraged by night were they not so starved.

Those twelve elk now wending their way back up the mountain were not only survivors of the winter, but also survivors of numerous great herds of elk that had once lived in the Rocky Mountains and throughout the whole northern portion of the United States and southern Canada. Three centuries ago elk had been plentiful in the wooded areas of the East Coast.

Had the colonists bothered to ask, they might have avoided some mistakes in semantics with which we are plagued to this day. So named by the colonists, the American "Indians"—who called themselves Algonquin and Mohawk (tribes of the Iroquois nation)—had named the two largest members of the Western Hemisphere's deer family "moose" and "wapiti."

By the sixteenth century, moose had been hunted to near extinction in most of Europe, but still existed in Norway where they were and still are called "elk." The wapiti of America had never been in Europe, but were distant cousins of the European red stag. When the colonists stepped off their ships, having never

13

seen Indians, moose, elk, wapiti, Algonquin, Mohawk, or Iroquois before, they proceeded to misname everything in sight.

No doubt the tribes of the Iroquois nation shook their heads in disbelief at such hardheads who just wouldn't listen. Had they known that many of the colonists were in America for the simple reason that they'd been thrown out of Europe for not listening over there either, the Iroquois might have understood. And had they known all that, the Iroquois would surely have banded together sooner and not have allowed those foolish English a foothold on what was then their continent.

At any rate, once established, the colonists proceeded to push wapiti, moose, and even Iroquois westward—and all to near extinction.

Something like 65 million years before the early colonists bumbled ashore onto this continent, the bald mountain home of Harold, the bull elk, first pushed its flat head above a vast sea now known as the western troughs of the Mesozoic era. Huge quantities of silt were eroded from the Canadian Shield and deposited in the Sundance Sea to the east and north of Colorado in the Dakotas, Nebraska, and Wyoming. The tremendous weight of all this silt caused the thin floor of the western troughs to erupt, thus creating the Rocky Mountain range.

Harold's mountain, lying on the western side of the Rocky Mountain divide, was simply pushed upward without any volcanic eruptions or other violent spasms. As a result of its relatively gentle birth, this bald mountain and others like it were host to the evolution of grass, which preserved its flat top from erosion; and as the grass evolved, so did the grass-eating mammals, such as camels, horses, antelope, and a type of deer. The "mule" deer that evolved in North America were of a different genus and species than the elk and moose who later came here as immigrants—the same way that all humans arrived on this continent.

The Pleistocene Ice Age, which followed the Mesozoic Era,

caused great changes in climate, from tropical to temperate, from humid to arid. Species that had evolved in the once tropical Rocky Mountain area had three choices: adapt, migrate, or become extinct. The polar ice caps formed during the Pleistocine Ice Age consumed so much of the earth's water that all ocean levels fell by approximately 300 feet, exposing the shallow straits of the Bering Sea.

Anthropologists believe it was over this "land bridge" that many of the first immigrants came to the American continent. Ancestors of the European elk, red stag, bison, and man (now respectively called moose, elk, buffalo, and Indian) all crossed to America via the Bering land bridge. This same bridge is also believed to have been used by "migrants" such as the horse and the camel, who left North America and became extinct there until later reintroduced by man. For some peculiar reason the American mule deer remained in America and, equally strange, the Aurochs remained in Europe where it was to be domesticated.

Many lexicographers have confused the aurochs with the bison, probably because the ancestor of cattle (aurochs or *Bos bonasus*) is of the same order and family as is that of the bison, or wisent *(Bison bonasus)*, but is of a different genus and species.

Two of the newcomers to America adapted marvelously. The bison enjoyed the open plain, and the wapiti (elk) thrived where grass and wood merged. Man followed wherever game was plentiful and easy to take. Game was never very easy to take atop the bald mountain.

A change in climate brought about after the Pleistocene Ice Age altered this particular mountain. To adapt to life there, grazing animals had to adopt an annual migration up and down its flanks because of the harsh winters. Over the years the elk and the mule deer had come to understand this. Charles and Jim Radson would soon learn also. The mountain, benevolent in its youth, now alternated annually between bounty and brutality.

Chapter 4

After some grave misgivings, Sue Radson, Jim's wife, had come to love her new life on the CR Ranch. At first, Sue dismissed the fateful decision made by her husband, Jim, and John Colvin to become partners in a cattle ranch, as the product of an evening's drinking. As their plans began to jell, however, Sue began to worry. The day the two land barons burst in upon her, waving their purchase papers, she was horrified! Bidding farewell to her suburban neighbors on June 25, 1974 was a heart-rending affair.

The actual transition from life in the suburbs of Denver to the ranch happened so smoothly that she still could not believe it. Noon meals and coffee breaks with her husband and two boys turned out to be much more enjoyable than the daytime company of the neighborhood wives back in Denver. Perhaps the greatest change for the good that Sue noticed was in Jim. During his carpentry days back in Denver, Jim had often come home bearing a six-pack of beer, which he then would consume before the television screen.

Here on the CR he seldom thought of either television or beer. Evenings were spent poring through breeding journals, a cup of cold coffee nearby. The town of Eagle's one-channel TV relay produced such fitful bursts of mediocrity that even the boys quickly transferred their loyalty to the horses, cattle, tractor, and pickup truck. The Radsons' new home, which was the best of the three ranch homes purchased, became a great joy to Sue as winter set in. Cozy and warm, it had a large kitchen, two bedrooms, and a living room with a huge stone fireplace.

The thing that Sue especially enjoyed was the view from her kitchen window. Back in Denver her kitchen window offered a perfect view of the neighbors' garage wall — ten feet away. The view from the ranch window was spectacular! It looked out across the pasture toward the now snow-covered mountaintop looming above the wooded slopes. Colorado winter with its bright snow, clear blue sky, and mountain greenery could only be described in the most superlative of terms.

Looking out through her window one January morning, Sue was the first to see the small band of elk edging out of the woods toward the fenced-in stacks of hay across the pasture, and it was she who noticed the big old bull elk and named him Harold.

The Radson boys had wanted their father to shoot the old bull and have his antlers mounted above the fireplace, but Jim declined, saying, "Old Harold is needed for the herd. Besides that, it's not elk season, and furthermore he'd be too tough to eat." As the winter wore on, and Jim could see that the hay supply would be ample for the cow herd, he would even toss out a little hay at the edge of the woods for the elk.

Throughout the winter, Sue had also noticed a rangy old beef cow who was always off by herself on the same corner of the pasture frequented by the elk, and had given her the name "Old Maude."

One of the peculiar happenings in this world since man assumed control of it (or rather assumed he had control of it) was that nature selected those to survive from among the ones who could take care of themselves, whereas man, the new self-anointed ruler of the planet, selected survivors from among those who depended on him for their existence. A good herdsman would have culled Old Maude long ago for no other reason than her complete lack of any herding instinct. Maude owed her very existence to Jim Radson's lack of experience, and to her previous owner's advancing age. Her inability to stay with the herd was the reason she would calve in June rather than early May like the rest of the herd.

The previous August, Maude had found a small meadow about two thirds of the way up the side of the mountain, which she preferred to the mountaintop above the tree line where the rest of the cows spent the summer. The little meadow had been created by a mudslide some years past. The slide had been caused by a spring at the upper end of the meadow, which had flowed profusely during a wet period some fifty years ago. The ground below the spring had become saturated, and, lubricated by the spring's water, it simply slid down the mountainside, destroying all the trees in its path—a natural sort of erosion. Grass soon established itself on the bare earth, and now the trees were again pushing back in along the edges of the meadow. The spring still flowed, but, due to the drought of the past few years, it practically dried up in the fall. The elk herd used the spring frequently. During dry periods they would scrape the earth away to form depressions for the water to collect so they could drink.

The meadow itself was hidden from the ranch below by the berm, or bench of earth, left by the slide. The slide meadow, lying between two finger ridges running up the mountainside, was well protected from the wind and was accessible only by two narrow and difficult game trails down each ridge. In her meanderings, Maude had discovered the meadow and came to use it frequently. She happened to be there in early September when the Radsons had made their first fall roundup. Later, in early October, they caught her on the mountaintop and drove her down to the winter pasture, where she was bred by Black Hercules and remained throughout the winter of '74–75.

Maude's habit of keeping to herself caught Sue Radson's attention and caused her to look for the old cow each morning as she prepared breakfast. On the day of Charles's birth, Sue looked out her window and saw Jim returning to the house.

Looks like Maude's finally has had her calf, thought Sue as she turned from the window to the stove. *Jim's on his way back so I'd better get busy. Some of those neighborhood gossips back in Denver would just die if they knew what breakfast was like up here,* she thought, smiling to herself. *I could never have imagined frying steak for breakfast.* During Jim's carpentry days, Sue would get up first, make coffee, and start to pack his lunch before trying to awaken him.

I could always tell how the job was going for Jim by the way he behaved in the morning, she thought. *If he were helping build a fancy home where they expected good workmanship, he'd be up on time and want to eat breakfast. If the only work he could find was on tract housing, he'd get up late and leave the house angry without breakfast. And I'd have thrown up if I'd had to fry beefsteak in the morning,* Sue laughed.

Here on the ranch Jim's new habit of getting up at dawn for a pre-breakfast inspection of the calving pastures gave Sue time to wake up slowly in bed, a luxury she used to imagine only the rich could afford. She had just finished setting the table as she heard Jim muttering to himself out in the entry, and sensed something was wrong.

"Can you imagine that! Old Maude just had a red calf," he said as he came into the kitchen with bare feet and jeans wet to the knees from the morning dew. "I can't believe it. Last fall, after we caught her sneaking around on the mountaintop, I put her in the breeding pen and saw Hercules breed her myself. He wouldn't have done it if she hadn't been in heat. That old cow couldn't have been close to any other bull that I know of!"

Jim sat down at the table and poured the coffee. "An Angus bull crossed with a Hereford cow is supposed to make a black calf with a white face one hundred percent of the time."

Sue brought the food to the table, sat down, and said, " Was one of the Hereford bulls with her anytime?"

"No," said Jim. "They were all over in the other pasture with the herd. Anyhow, I remember letting Hercules in with her."

"I doubt that Old Maude is much of a Hereford, you know," said Sue thoughtfully.

"I'll bet that's it! I'm going to cull that old bag as soon as she weans her calf. You know she stood me off from that calf! I really believe she'd have fought me if I'd have touched that darned calf. I could see it was a bull calf anyhow, so I'll castrate him before we drive the cattle up to the summer pasture, and next fall I'll ship Maude and her calf off to market. Oh well, when John and I bought this spread we knew we'd have to upgrade the stock. That's why we bought Hercules."

By the time Sue and Jim had finished their breakfast, the boys were up and clamoring for pancakes. The conversation shifted to a fence-mending project that Jim had planned for himself and the boys, and Sue temporarily forgot to ask Jim about a letter she had received from her cousin back in Minnesota, asking if they cared if he came out hunting in the fall.

Radson was not the only one concerned with the condition of the CR fences. Old Maude was feeling a restless springtime urge to climb the mountain. It was the same urge that had caused the elk to leave the valley in May.

As soon as Charles gained strength in his wobbly legs, Maude began to patrol the winter-pasture fence. Three days after Charles' birth she found a place where heavy snow had toppled a spruce tree across the fence; there she made good her escape, coaxing Charles to wiggle beneath the barbed wire.

Jim and the boys discovered the broken fence shortly after the pair escaped. Fresh tracks of a cow and calf etched sharply in the damp earth, plus a few strands of red hair hanging from the lower barbed wire, told Jim who was missing.

"Dang that Old Maude! She got away with her calf before we had a chance to cut him," Jim cursed, and then said to his sons, "You guys be sure to remind me to get rid of both of them when we pick them up this fall."

CHAPTER 5

It had taken some doing for Maude to coax Charles through the fence and into the woods bordering the winter pasture. Once through the fence and into the woods, Charles was seized with fear. This new world that he had just entered was different; it was dark and cool, and smelled foreign. Even the earth he trod felt different. He took each of his first few steps on the soft, spongy carpet of spruce needles with great caution, first smelling the ground, and then gently placing his forefoot upon it, while Maude impatiently urged him on.

Back in the early days of ranching, cowboys often watched new calves with amusement as they entered strange surroundings. The calves would place each hoof tenderly down as if they had sore feet; the cowboys got to calling new calves "tenderfeet," and eventually started calling anyone new to the West a "tenderfoot."

Charles, having finally lost his fear of the woods, followed his mother closely as she started traveling straight up a finger ridge leading up the mountainside. Pausing often to let Charles rest and nurse, Maude made her way toward a mountain meadow known only to her and a few others.

On the morning of the second day of her escape, she found the game trail she was looking for, which led off to the left across a steep, slippery shale slide. With great concern for young Charles, she slowly picked her way across the narrow trail, stopping often to watch his progress. Once across, the trail widened and became less difficult. The last quarter mile to her hidden meadow led through a heavy stand of large black spruce. Fresh tracks and scents converging on the trail told Maude that she would find some old acquaintances at the meadow. Sure enough, as they emerged from the spruce several head of elk looked up in surprise — the same group that had survived the winter on Jim Radson's largesse. The elk had been taking their ease across the meadow and didn't hear Maude and Charles approaching because of the noise made by the cavorting elk calves, which disguised whatever noise Maude and Charles made on the trail. Within minutes Maude and the elk recognized each other, not exactly as old friends, but rather as old acquaintances who meant each other no harm. The elk resumed their rumination and play while Maude grazed her way up to the spring, Charles at her side.

The birth of six new calves had boosted the number of elk in Harold's herd to eighteen. The only claim Harold had to the group was that he'd sired most of the calves. As is the case in most elk herds, there was a lead cow who decided where and when they should go. It was only during the rut, or mating season, that Harold bullied them about. Mostly, whenever they traveled, he was well to the rear; the habit of being a rear guard had saved his life more than once. Hunters on stand had fired on the first elk they saw, only to watch Harold escape, his royal antlers still intact.

Harold and the two other young bull elk now appeared more comical than regal. Having shed their antlers in early March, they were now in the process of growing new sets. Antlers grew inside, nourished by a velvety skin. This June morning their antlers were just velvet-covered stalks with a bulbous knob wherever a new fork was about to appear. At this stage, antlers were very tender; the bulls were quite docile and were careful not to bump them against anything. Mostly, the bulls grazed peacefully and slept much until August, when the itch of the shedding velvet goaded them into frenetic activity. By September they would be dueling with each other.

By far the most popular place in the meadow was the berm at the lower end of the clearing. It was the only reasonably level spot with a good view of the whole meadow. Maude and the cow elk would often bed down there throughout the midday. Elk and cattle — ruminants both — would alternately lie on the ground chewing their cud, and stand contentedly while their calves nursed. The calves would sleep, nurse, and romp about the berm bench. Charles, having never seen another calf like himself, gamboled with the elk calves as if he were one of them.

The elk remained at the meadow nearly two weeks after Charles and Maude arrived. One day, feeling the urge to climb up above the timberline, the lead cow elk left, the entire herd in tow. Charles couldn't understand why Maude didn't go along.

Maude would also go up above the timberline in the middle of July, but for now she was content to remain on her now private meadow. With plenty of grass and water, she viewed the little meadow as a fine place to rear her calf. The departure of the elk, however, left poor Charles with no playmates. Maude was not the playful type, and either ignored or reprimanded Charles for his attempts to play.

The other permanent residents of the meadow — chipmunks, pine squirrels, mountain jays, and a pair of snowshoe rabbits — were much too small to be playmates for the lonesome calf, but they soon recognized him for what he was, a nosy youngster, and ceased crying in alarm whenever he approached. Twice a day an American eagle would coast across the meadow in search of prey. Even before his shadow drifted onto the grass, the jays and squirrels would sound an alarm and then dash for cover.

Early one morning, one of the snowshoe hares tarried too long in the open over a clump of clover. Unfortunately for him, he was exposed just as the eagle glided onto the scene. The sharp-eyed jays and squirrels sounded their alarm and dashed for cover, while the eagle, in a rush of feathers and talons, caught the hare a scant fifteen yards from the astonished Charles. The shrieks of terror and pain as the eagle made his kill, and the smell of blood, were forever etched on the young calf's mind.

Charles thus learned to use the eyes of the little sentinels of the woods as well as he used his own. Something in his genetic makeup caused him to understand the difference between the idle chatter and the alarm cries of the small animals. Charles was starting to learn the skills necessary for survival.

Chance and his mother's maverick qualities also had a great deal to do with his survival and with his chances of passing his genes on to future generations. Had Maude not found the gap in the fence caused by the tree that had been toppled by the previous winter's snow and thus escaped the CR Ranch, Charles would have been castrated by Jim Radson within the first few days of his life.

Charles, you might say, had been born to survive.

CHAPTER 6

September 1975 was upon Smitty long before he was ready for it. The hunting trip planned by his pal, Bob Bine, to which Smitty had rather absent-mindedly agreed, was about to become a fact. But Bob, the eternal optimist, had some anxious moments in late June. During a bit of horseplay at work, he'd severed the tendons of two fingers of his right hand.

Life on the hog-cut line became so monotonous that almost any diversion was welcome. Tossing scraps of meat around the place was forbidden. Anyone guilty of it was supposed to be fined by the union and temporarily suspended from work. Foremen were required to report any such infraction, but, even if they saw it happen, they usually neglected to do so.

Once Bob and Smitty had carved (or pulled, as was the common jargon on the line) the loin from the carcass, they shoved the loins onto a chute that led down to a table where two other men trimmed the excess fat from the loins. Koehler, one of the trimmers, had become an expert at tossing meat without getting caught. He would snip off a bit of fat, stick it onto the tip of his knife, bend the blade back with his other hand, and then catapult it with unerring accuracy onto the back of some unfortunate coworker's neck.

While trying to catch one of these tosses, Bob accidentally struck the back of his hand against his spare knife. Bob was led off to first aid, his hand wrapped in a dirty and bloody towel. The company doctor neatly fished the tendons out with a pair of forceps and fastened them securely back together. Three weeks off work and five more weeks of light duty found Bob back on the line pulling loins again.

During the first break of the day on which he returned to work, Bob found Smitty crouched on his haunches as usual in the rest area near the latrine. "Hey, Smitty! How's it going?" burst out Bob as usual.

"Same as always," replied Smitty. "How's the hand?"

"Darned near hacked my trigger finger off!" Bine said as he lit his cigarette. "Actually, two of the fingers are a little stiff yet, but they're coming along. I've got a rubber ball that I squeeze to improve things."

"Are you still planning on that elk-hunting trip?" asked Smitty.

"What do you mean, 'are you still planning?' We – are – going, and I want seventy-five bucks from you to send in for licenses this week!"

"Okay, I'll bring it tomorrow. My wife was wondering if I was really going or just having another pipe dream," Smitty replied.

"I heard from my cousin, and we're in; thousands of acres to hunt on. Oh, crap! It's time to get back to the damned line again. Next break you've got to hear about the pickup camper that I bought last week for our trip! Tell you about it later," said Bob, flipping his half-smoked cigarette in the general direction of the ashtray.

"What a hell of a lousy job!" thought Smitty as he got up to go back to the line. "Can't even finish a conversation. It's always back to the line and the same damned crappy work.

That dumb Koehler and his horseplay, thought Smitty while heading back to his station. *But I suppose everyone has to do something to preserve his sanity while doing this idiotic work. Koehler sure is a sly old geezer to keep getting away with chucking fat around the place all these years. The trouble with that sort of horseplay is that often someone gets hurt.*

Once back on the line, Smitty picked up his knife, the conveyer again jerked into motion, and he resumed his usual robot-like motions.

Different people respond differently to boredom. Smitty's defense against it was simply to slow down his mental processes and sort of dream his way through the day's work. He woke up slowly in the morning, and didn't really come to until the day at the plant was nearly over. Once he'd concluded his boring work, Smitty began to come to life again. Usually, he went straight home for either a cup of coffee or a can of beer with his wife. Evenings were a time to plan, discuss finances, or just kid around. Unfortunately, over the past three years Smitty found it had become increasingly more difficult to converse with his wife upon returning from work. His two daughters came rushing home from school about the same time he arrived. More often than not, his wife was far more interested in the children's affairs than in whatever Smitty had learned at the plant.

Guess I really can't blame her much for that, thought Smitty as, with no thought of his physical actions, he drew his knife along the loin of another half of a hog's carcass slowly moving by. *What in the hell ever happens here at the plant? It seems like the only news around here is when someone gets careless and cuts himself.*

Smitty then found himself recalling the day old Stokey had stabbed himself. Stokey was a loin trimmer just like Koehler, and trimmed the loins that Bob Bine pulled, just as Koehler did for Smitty. Koehler and Stokey worked at the same table, which lay between the twin conveyer lines. Both were in their mid-fifties, and, from the love of their beer, both had become florid-faced and paunchy. Shortly, someone with an easier job would retire, and Stokey, with plenty of seniority, would probably move up into the vacated spot. Smitty, with more seniority than Bob, would then be allowed to bid for and probably get Stokey's job—even though Smitty was sure he didn't want to spend the next two or three years standing across the table from Koehler.

Koehler had an ornery streak. Perhaps a half dozen times in the past two years Smitty had seen him sneak Stokey's knives and blunt them against the stainless-steel table, just for the sake of watching poor old Stokey sweat while trying to trim loins with a dull knife for the next sixty-five minutes. Stokey himself wasn't a bad sort; he just seemed to be a blabbermouth, constantly talking, always spinning some windy old yarn.

Stokey can always turn a short story into a long one, thought Smitty. *Probably, that's the way he's kept from going completely daft doing this rotten work. Bine's never-ending dreams of some new hunting or fishing trip, Stokey' constant prattling, and Koehler' dirty tricks— probably are things they do just to stay sane on this idiotic job.*

Even though Smitty didn't realize it, his personal relief from boredom was philosophy. Somewhat taciturn himself, he watched others and tried to figure out why they did whatever. Smitty should have finished college and become a psychologist.

Thinking of Stokey and Koehler made Smitty recall something that had happened two years before. Old Stokey had been telling a particularly long tale and had fallen behind in his work. Koehler, of course, wouldn't help him catch up.

For obvious reasons, workers who regularly use knives are required to wear a metallic mesh glove on the hand opposite the knife. The loin trimmer's usual process was to reach across the table with his gloved hand and pull another loin toward himself, then, with two or three deft strokes of the knife, remove all the excess fat from the loin. Stokey had fallen behind and Koehler was laughing at him, so, to speed up the process, Stokey started hooking loins toward himself with his knife. Unfortunately, he hooked a soft loin, the knife cut through it, and Stokey stabbed himself up the nose.

29

Smitty recalled how he nearly passed out at the sight of old Stokey standing there holding his split nose in amazement as the blood gushed. Someone shut the line down, and foremen came running and cursing, but the line stayed down until Stokey was led off to the doctor and his blood had been hosed down the drain.

Any shutdown of the line automatically started up the plant grapevine. Within minutes the whole place was buzzing about how some fool stabbed himself in the snout! *What sort of crazy people would find that funny?* Smitty thought, even though he had gone home and tried to tell his wife the story in a humorous vein.

It was thus that Smitty spent the following sixty-five-minute work period and all others like it throughout the month of September. During each break Bob Bine would be almost bubbling over with enthusiasm about the upcoming hunting trip, while Smitty mostly just listened . And so it went, until the time came to leave for Colorado. Then, Smitty was forced to stay up most of the night before their departure, collecting his hunting gear.

CHAPTER 7

What a dumb way to begin a vacation, mused Smitty while trying to relax his right foot, which had become cramped from pressing the accelerator the past four hours. *Almost every working day I get up to drive to work before sunrise, and here I am, on my vacation, again driving before dawn. At least I'll be able to watch the sunrise today, and I won't be locked up inside that damned plant!*

Smitty and Bob had left home right after work Thursday evening and had alternately driven the truck and slept in the camper throughout the night. Hunting season would open Saturday morning, so they had taken Friday off to travel to Colorado. They planned to arrive at the CR Ranch about noon on Friday to assess the hunting situation. Bob had driven most of the evening, smoking one cigarette after another and talking excitedly and incessantly about the upcoming hunt. About eleven P.M. Smitty had crawled back into the camper and slept intermittently for two hours, when Bob had become too sleepy to continue driving.

I wonder what Nebraska looks like? Smitty thought. *Here I am farther away from home than I've ever been, and I still haven't seen anything. Maybe it'll be daylight through here when we're on our way back home.* Looking back through the rear window of the truck into the camper, Smitty could see Bine still asleep. *Too bad Bob's not awake and driving now,* thought Smitty as he tried changing radio stations again. *He really likes this country-western music and I sure*

31

am getting sick of it. Seems like that's all a person can find on the air this early in the morning.

"Enough is enough!" Smitty said aloud, switching the radio off. "When we get closer to Denver we should be able to find something else, maybe even a little light classical music, but by then Bob will be awake and won't want to listen to that either. Those guys back in the plant would laugh their heads off if they knew I enjoyed classical music and that I even attended the ballet occasionally back when I was in college."

With the arrival of dawn Smitty was driving twenty-five miles east of Sterling, Colorado, on Interstate 74, which had been parallel and just to the south of the Platte River across western Nebraska. Throughout the gloomy dark of that portion of the night when he had been forced to drive, he had noticed lights from farms along the river on his right; to the left, or south, nothing. The dim light of early morning finally allowed Smitty a view of the south fork of the Platte.

So that's what the South Platte looks like, thought Smitty. *It's just a little old meandering creek in the middle of a big flat valley. Looks like when it floods it gets pretty wide.*

Recalling some of the Western history he had read caused Smitty to marvel how, without his ever having even seen it, he'd traveled overnight along the same trail that had cost early Mormon and Oregon settlers more than a month of toil and hardship.

I'll have to remember to tell Bob about the Mormons that traveled this trail afoot, no horses or oxen, all their possessions in pushcarts. He probably won't believe me anyhow, he thought with a grin. *Sure hope he wakes up before we get to Sterling, as I'm getting tired and hungry.*

Breakfast in Sterling—where Bob Bine disbelieved Smitty's story of the Mormons and their pushcarts—and lunch in Denver were followed by a late-afternoon arrival at the CR Ranch, where Bob's cousin, Susan, and her husband, Jim Radson, greeted them pleasantly.

In view of their late arrival, Jim pointed out that there wasn't enough sunlight left for a scouting trip up the bald mountain behind the ranch. In place of scouting, Jim gave them an invitation to supper and a tour of the ranch buildings and corrals. During the tour Jim proudly pointed out the CR cattle and calves, which they'd just brought down from the mountain top pasture. Of particular pride to him were Black Hercules and some of his white-faced black offspring. (He conveniently forgot about Hercules's red calf and its obstinate mother who'd again given him the slip during the fall roundup.)

Both Bob and Smitty were disappointed to learn that Jim wouldn't be available to hunt with them for the next three days, as he had to sort out and sell all the calves that would not be held as breeding stock.

After supper was finished, Jim brought out his maps of the CR Ranch and spread them on the table. He pointed out areas above the timberline where he'd often seen the elk herd, and the trail used to drive the cattle to the top of the mountain. The CR holdings consisted of the mountain's northern slope and part of its eastern slope, which Jim claimed would be the most accessible to them. The western slopes were covered with heavy timber owned by the Federal Department of Forestry, and, due to the lack of access roads, would be impossible for them to hunt and return to their camper daily.

Unfortunately, three of the four CR horses would be needed for cutting the calves from the herd for the next three days. Once the calves had been sorted out and shipped, Jim and the horses would be available to join the hunt or to pack the elk that Bob and Smitty presumably would have shot by then back down the mountain.

The relief of not having to ride horses eleven miles up the steep cattle trail pointed out by Radson showed so openly on the faces of the two nimrods (neither of whom rode) that Jim didn't feel bad that he couldn't provide transportation up and down the bald mountain. He did, however, point out a more direct and steep route leading up some finger ridges from the east, which he knew of but hadn't traveled. Going upward from a campsite near a government reservoir on the east slope of the mountain, it would be only about a five-mile hike to the top.

That a power transmission line also ran along the lower east side of the mountain gave Bob and Smitty more relief, in that, should they become lost, they needed only hike down the eastern slope until they intersected the power line that would lead them back to their camp.

Full of information, anticipation, high spirits, and CR beef, the two dauntless hunters bade the Radsons good night and headed toward the reservoir campsite by way of a twisted country road, having promised to return for supper three days hence, when the horses and Jim's "expert" guide service would be available. Upon arriving at the campsite they were disappointed to find another party of hunters drunkenly cavorting about a huge campfire.

After having attempted conversation with the other group about the hunting, Bob and Smitty gave up in disgust and turned in for the evening. Bob immediately fell into a deep and sonorous sleep. Kept awake by the drunken boastful shouting of the other hunters and by Bob's snores, Smitty soon developed a sinking sensation concerning the impending hunt.

Thinking back over the happenings of that evening, Smitty realized that they would be heading up a mountain over a route prescribed but never traveled by their guide, Jim, who'd never hunted elk before, and in the company of a bunch of drunks. Smitty felt sure, as he fell asleep, that this hunting trip would be unsuccessful.

THE HUNT

CHAPTER 8

On the first morning of the hunt, Smitty was pulled grumbling from his sleeping bag at four-thirty A.M. by Bob, who was as bubbling as the coffeepot that he had on the gas stove. Bob's plan was to get an early start up the mountain, thus beating the other hunters to the elk.

In less time than it took Smitty to shake the sleep from his head and don his clothes, Bob managed to boil the coffeepot over and burn the bacon. That accomplished, he then turned the stove's heat down too low and started scrambling eggs in cold grease.

"Remind me to fix supper," said Smitty as he tried to finish his breakfast of burned bacon, greasy eggs, and yucky coffee.

Bob, who'd already wolfed his breakfast, and was concocting some crude sandwiches for their lunch, said, "Hurry up! We don't want those other guys ahead of us, do we?"

"Fat chance," replied Smitty. "Considering all the boozing they were doing last night, they'll probably still be sleeping at noon."

Ignoring Smitty's remark, Bob said, "I figure just as soon as there's enough light to see, we should head out. Each of us ought to pick a ridge and work our way up to the timberline. Then you could go around to the right, and I'll go around to the left. Okay?"

"Sounds all right to me," replied Smitty as he felt his stomach growling its disapproval of what had been forced upon it.

"Cripes! Where did I pack my rifle shells?" cried out Bob, rummaging about in the bottom of his duffel bag. "Here they are! Lemme see now, have I got everything? Compass, lunch, matches, first-aid kit—what else?"

"Toilet paper," said Smitty, rubbing his complaining stomach.

"Well, that's it. I guess I have everything. Don't you think we'd better get moving soon?" asked Bob, who'd paid not the slightest attention to what Smitty had said.

"Ye gods! It won't be daylight for almost two hours," exclaimed Smitty. "Let's wash the dishes. I'd sure hate to come back this evening and be forced to look at this mess you've made."

"Oh, all right, you wash and I'll dry. Tonight *you* can cook and I'll do all the dishes," said Bob, somewhat chagrined.

Having completed the morning chores, they hoisted packs and rifles, then started out southward along the power line, leaving behind the sound of the other hunters coughing and cursing as they struggled out of sleeping bags. They walked nearly half a mile before Smitty picked a likely finger ridge to ascend. Bob decided to take the next ridge; hopefully, they would meet somewhere above the timberline.

Three hours later, Smitty found himself only partway up the mountain. *Back home,* thought Smitty as he paused for a rest, *four miles doesn't seem very far, but here, almost straight up and in such dense forest, it's a terrible distance.*

For the past half-hour he'd expected to reach the timberline any moment, but upon pausing at nine-thirty A.M., he found himself in a more heavily forested area than ever. The trees about him were large and mature. A windstorm several years before had blown some of them into a wildly tangled mess. Logs were crisscrossed in every direction like a gigantic game of jackstraws.

I'll bet I've gone a hundred yards at a time crawling over logs without ever touching ground. Such a waste, thought Smitty while relaxing on a fallen tree. *I can see enough down timber from where I'm sitting*

37

to build twenty homes. I can't imagine why the forestry service didn't allow it to be harvested.

The air at this altitude was so thin that Smitty found it impossible to maintain his usual pace. Upon first starting up the ridge he was surprised to find himself completely winded after only 500 yards. He later learned that, by climbing more slowly, he would be able to continue with only an occasional pause.

I wonder how old Bob is making out? At the rate he smokes cigarettes I'll bet he's really winded.

Recalling something he'd read in the past, Smitty pulled out a book of matches from his pocket and lit one. The match flared and then burned with but a tiny flame.

Not much oxygen up here, Smitty thought, realizing he was about to toss the still-burning match onto the ground. *Stupid! This area is as dry as tinder.*

The elevation where he was now sitting at ten A.M., 7,000 feet and two thirds of the way up, was covered with a carpet of dry twigs and pine needles, which crackled and rustled, loudly announcing his progress up the mountainside. The temperature at daylight back in camp had been just above freezing, and as he'd climbed and the day progressed the temperature climbed also. About eight-thirty he'd shed his woolen hunting coat, and on this pause had removed his long johns and stored them in his pack.

Man, it must be almost eighty degrees out. This sort of hunting is sure different than the deer hunting back in Minnesota, with its snow and sub-zero temperatures. This just can't be normal weather for this country, Smitty mused.

As he shouldered his pack and rifle preparatory to resuming his climb, Smitty reasoned, *Before long I should be breaking out of this heavy timber and getting up toward the timberline. Maybe by then there'll be a chance to sneak up on some elk. So far, if there were any around, they'd have heard me coming half a mile away.*

About eleven-thirty Smitty noticed the timber was thinning into more dwarfed and stunted timberline growth, and by noon he broke out onto the bald mountaintop. Here he crossed a rusty barbed-wire fence that the previous CR owners had built and that Jim Radson would have to repair if he wanted to contain his cattle on the mountaintop next summer.

Well, I wonder where Bob is? Smitty pondered. *I'll wait here awhile, eat lunch, and see if he shows up.*

Opening his pack, he extracted a brown paper bag and, upon viewing its dry crumbling contents, observed, *At least the view from up here compensates for this miserable mess that Bob made for lunch.*

Millions of years before, when the Rockies slowly inched upward from the sea floor, the mountain on which Smitty sat in solitude had managed to rear its head high enough above the surrounding mountains to acquire an excellent view of the Rocky Mountain divide, which lay some sixty miles eastward. On the previous day, when Bob and Smitty had crossed the divide, all was encased in the gray of a cloud bank parked atop the divide. This was Smitty's first exposure to the rugged beauty of the Rockies; now hunched down on a rock outcropping, munching the dry crumbs of his lunch, he was struck by the beauty of what lay before him.

This moment makes the whole trip worthwhile, beamed Smitty as he dug his camera and binoculars out of his pack. Having taken several photos, he put the camera away and began to glass the immediate area with his binoculars, hoping to see Bob emerge from the timberline. Alternately scanning the area where he expected Bob, and trying to choke down the miserable sandwich Bob had manufactured, made him wish he'd brought water along.

"I'd give a dollar for a glass of cold water," he sighed, turning his binoculars north. "I'll bet Bob probably hurried straight up his ridge and dashed off south just like he was back home running to the cafeteria in the plant at noontime."

Giving up on Bob, Smitty turned his attention to the north. Some reddish brown lumps on a grassy point about a half-mile away caught his eye. Smitty focused his binoculars onto the spot. Elk! he realized with a start.

With growing excitement he began to plan his stalk: drop back down to the timberline and go about halfway there, then out to the edge for another look. Assuming that his hunting partner had arrived at the timberline ahead of him and had gone off to the south, Smitty started after the elk alone. It took almost half an hour to move to a position nearer the herd. Cautiously moving up to the end of a small ravine, he crawled out and had another look with the binoculars. Sure enough, the brown spots were an elk herd, fifteen in number. One had a tremendous set of antlers.

That's probably Harold, the big old bull elk that the Radson boys were talking about, he thought.

Having never seen elk before, the sight of Harold's small herd caused Smitty's heart to pound with excitement. He had to force himself to be calm enough to figure out a plan of action. The elk were bedded down on the edge of another small ravine running up the mountain. At this time of day air currents would be rising up the ravine, so another stalk back down to the timberline and up the ravine would risk giving his scent to the elk before he could get within shooting distance.

A safer route to the herd would be from above. By taking advantage of several depressions and by crawling the last hundred yards on his stomach, he figured he would end up 200 yards uphill from the elk and, most important, downwind. Caching his pack, Smitty began his final stalk.

Thirty minutes later he lay on a small knoll about 600 yards from the herd, looking for a concealed route toward them. Harold, the only antlered elk present, lay on the far side of the herd.

The rut must be on, Smitty thought, *and the old boy's driven all the other bulls away.*

As he watched, old Harold rose stiffly from his bed, cast a baleful eye about, and then bugled out his challenge to whatever foolish male elk might be within hearing distance. "Pweee-pwee! Pweee-pwee!" followed by a couple of short grunts.

"So that's what elk bugling sounds like," Smitty whispered. *If I had an elk call and knew how to use it, now would be a perfect chance. A couple challenge toots on the call and I'd bet Harold would run right over here ready to fight.*

Harold bellowed a couple more challenges, "Pweee-pwee!"

Just then from behind him, Smitty heard another sound, a faint droning, which grew louder.

Looking back over his shoulder, Smitty gritted his teeth and muttered, "An airplane! What the hell is an airplane doing here, and down so close to the ground?"

The small plane, a yellow Piper Cub, passed almost directly over Smitty at an altitude of 500 feet; then, upon spotting the elk, it banked sharply and dove at the herd. The elk immediately jumped up and dashed for the safety of the woods below.

"Dammit!" cried Smitty as he drew up on one knee, trying to catch Harold in the telescope of his rifle. "Six hundred yards and running! Not a chance! That damned airplane! Damn, damn, damn!"

The plane made one more pass at the elk, forcing them to jump over the fence and plunge on down the timber-covered ridge and out of Smitty's sight.

"Well, it looks like there's nothing left to do but follow them on down that ridge." Retrieving his pack, he again used his binoculars to scan the area where he thought to see Bob. "Still no sign of him. Either he got on top ahead of me and didn't wait, or else he never made it all the way up. If I don't get moving, there'll be precious little time left to try to track that herd and still make it back to camp before dark."

Returning to the place where the elk had jumped the fence,

Smitty started trailing them down the ridge. Their tracks showed him that the herd, after running down the ridge for a half-mile, had ceased running, then milled about for a bit before regrouping. Following the tracks even farther he discovered the herd had picked up and followed a game trail leading straight down the ridge. After nearly another mile the trail came onto an outcropping of rocks sparsely covered with small spruce trees. Picking up the trail again below the outcropping, Smitty could find no fresh tracks.

Turning back and moving in ever widening circles, he spotted a branch probably broken by Harold's large antlers. Closer examination revealed more faint tracks leading north through an extremely thick stand of spruce. *It doesn't seem possible that fifteen elk could have made their way through here and have left such little sign,* thought Smitty, as he crept cautiously along. Continuing along the trail, he discovered that he was on a separate and smaller ridge leading down and to the north.

Without realizing it, Smitty had discovered the back door to Old Maude's favorite place, hidden by the thick spruce forest. This was the trail most often used by Maude and the elk to gain access; it entered the slide meadow from the south, just slightly below the spring at the upper end of the clearing. Unknown to Smitty, the elk herd was hidden from his view in a depression just above the earthen berm formed by the mud slide some years ago. Edging out into the open he noticed an old Hereford cow drinking from a spring at the upper end of the clearing. Just as he was about to step into the clearing, a red calf came gamboling up the hill and blundered straight into Smitty. Charles had been down with the elk herd in a vain attempt to get the calves to play, but by now all of the young elk had outgrown any playfulness.

Upon confronting Smitty, Charles immediately broke and ran across the meadow, closely followed by Maude. Together they dashed down the north edge of the clearing toward the other escape route, spooking the elk herd out the same route ahead of them.

When Smitty realized what was happening, he ran about twenty yards downhill, only to catch a glimpse of the last few elk disappearing into the woods, closely followed by Charles and his mother. The clatter of falling stones dislodged from the shale slide made Smitty realize that once more he'd lost his chance for an elk.

Standing dejectedly alone in the game trail, Smitty became aware of how thirsty he was and returned to the spring for a drink. Once refreshed, he walked around, realizing what a pleasant place the slide meadow really was. Descending to its lower end, Smitty discovered that both the reservoir where he and Bob were camped and the CR Ranch were visible to him while standing atop the berm. Due to the inclination of the mountainside, the entire meadow was hidden from below by the tree-covered face of the berm itself. He could also see that if he followed the escape trail across the slide to the next ridge, he could then proceed down to the power line and back to camp. With luck the elk might have headed down also.

Cautiously edging across the trail over the loose shale, he was amazed that at least one of the elk or cattle hadn't fallen onto the rocks below. Once clear of the slide, the trail angled up the side of the next ridge until it joined another trail, which led both up and down the ridge. Unfortunately for Smitty, the elk and the cattle had taken the trail leading up. Checking his watch, he realized that he was in danger of nightfall catching him on the mountainside, so he gave up pursuing the elk and headed toward camp. Following the ridge down, Smitty intersected the power line at the southwest corner of the Radsons' winter pasture. Hurrying south along the power line, Smitty barely made it back into camp before dark.

Approaching their camper in the cold late-evening gloom, he was heartened to see that Bob was already there. As Smitty entered the camper, Bob pointed out somewhat sheepishly that he had their supper almost ready to cook, but perhaps Smitty should do the actual cooking, in view of the horrible mess he'd created for breakfast. While Smitty prepared their evening meal, Bob mixed a couple of drinks and told how he had not been able to ascend the ridge he'd set out on that morning. It seems he'd run into a cliff that he couldn't climb. Smitty then related his experiences of the day. As they ate they laid plans for the next day's hunt. The plan that evolved was to ascend the same ridge Smitty had descended until they came to the trail leading across the shale slide. Once there, Bob was to cross to the meadow and then ascend the south ridge to the bald mountaintop. After waiting awhile, Smitty would then climb on up his ridge, hoping to push the elk out above the timberline—provided they had remained on the ridge overnight.

Finished with the meal, Bob started washing the dishes as he'd promised that morning, and Smitty decided to try talking with the other group of hunters. Four in number, they were passing a bottle of Jack Daniel's about a campfire again, but didn't seem quite as loud as they had been the night before. As Smitty approached he overheard one of them complaining that his lousy radio wasn't working, but he abruptly changed the subject when he noticed Smitty nearing the fire.

They hailed him with the usual "Any luck?" and then pressed the whiskey bottle on him. Smitty grimaced, took a drink from the bottle, and then told about how the airplane had spoiled his stalk on the elk herd that he'd seen above the timberline. It seemed curious to him that they didn't seem too surprised at the story, but wanted to know just which ridge he had last seen the elk on. Not wanting company on tomorrow's hunt, he gave them a rather vague answer. One, who appeared to be something of a leader, ventured a comment that, having been disturbed no more than that, the elk would probably be back up on the mountaintop the next morning. When asked about their luck, the leader laughed and said that his boys had been too hung-over to get very far up the mountain today, and that if they didn't get to bed soon, to-morrow might be a repeat. It seemed they had been coming to this same area for several years with pretty good success.

Noticing that Bob had finished his chores, Smitty yawned and told the other group that he was tired and was going to turn in. Returning to their camper, both crawled into their sleeping bags for the night. Smitty fell asleep almost instantly, but Bob, who was less tired, overheard the tail end of a conversation in the other hunting camp.

"I'll be damned if I'll work those ridges before ten in the morning," one of them said. "There's too many downdrafts in those coulees before that, and I'd probably splatter my ass all over the mountainside if I tried it."

"They're using a goddamned airplane for spotting elk;" said Bob aloud to the now sleeping Smitty.

CHAPTER 9

Breakfast on the second day's hunt was a grand improvement over that of the first. With Smitty now doing the cooking the food was much more edible.

As planned, they left camp just before daylight, followed the power line north to the first ridge above the corner of the CR winter pasture, and ascended it together. Shortly before ten, they reached the trail leading to Maude's meadow. "You mean I'm supposed to follow that lousy-looking trail across that shale slide?" asked Bob doubtfully.

"Just be careful and you'll be okay," Smitty replied. "Yesterday a whole herd of elk, an old cow, and her calf managed it on a dead run."

Together they checked the trails for tracks and found only those made the day before when Smitty and Charles had frightened the elk out of the meadow.

Watching Bob safely cross the perilous trail and disappear into the spruce, Smitty thought, *You'd never know there was a beautiful little meadow over there. It sure would be a great place for a cabin. Well now, I guess I've about an hour to wait here before Bob crosses the meadow, climbs the ridge up to the timberline, and chooses a stand. Chances are the elk kept on moving last night and aren't on this ridge anymore. Still, there's always that chance.*

As Smitty lay in the sun waiting for Bob to get into position, he had time to reflect on the hunt to date. *The whole trouble with this elk hunt seems to be the early season and this unusually warm weather. That plus the fact that our camp is way down there and the elk are clear to hell up there. Those elk will stay up high until deep snow forces them down. Cripes, it takes half a day just to climb to the top, and about the same to get back down again. Sure doesn't leave any time for hunting! Looks to me like we should have brought along some backpacking equipment and camped out up on top.*

When the time of waiting had passed, he hoisted his pack and started zigzagging his way up the ridge. This ridge, above the north entrance to the meadow, was almost identical to the two he'd been on the day before: stands of mature and fallen trees, followed by stands of new growth, finally thinning out into sparse timberline growth. On his way up he'd noticed tracks indicating that the elk had ceased running as they approached the timberline. Upon reaching the timberline, Smitty found that the elk had probably remained in the woods until dark, and then had grazed their way southward, toward where Bob was probably waiting. Once clear of the timber, Smitty hiked on over to Bob's position on the next ridge south.

As Smitty approached, Bob pulled out his cigarettes and exclaimed, "Didn't see a thing except for that old Hereford cow and calf you told me about. You must have pushed her out of the woods just ahead of you, because about twenty minutes ago I heard a racket over that way. I thought for sure it was elk, then I heard some noise in that scrub right over there. My old heart really started pounding! I had my rifle off safety and was ready to shoot, when out of the brush sneaks that durned cow and calf. If she'd been a bull elk I'd probably have died of fright anyhow. You know, she went right back down that trail that I just came up — probably went back to that little meadow, and I don't blame her, it's such a pretty place."

Smitty replied, "I think the elk went by here last night. What do you think we ought to do? It's already one-thirty."

47

"Can you find the ridge you came up yesterday?" asked Bob.

"Sure, it's about half a mile south of here."

"Then why don't we follow the timberline south awhile and get back to that ridge in time to get down off this mountain before dark. We sure don't want to try going down a ridge like I tried coming up yesterday. Might fall over a cliff in the dark," said Bob. "Besides that, I don't want to spend the night freezing up here with no sleeping bag."

"Let's get going then," Smitty replied. "We only ought to stay up here for two more hours."

The two started out southward, keeping down along the scrubby brush of the timberline, hoping to surprise the elk herd. They had gone about two miles when Bob stopped and asked, "Listen, do you hear an airplane?"

"I sure as hell do! Look down there, over that ridge. It's that same yellow Cub."

Just then they heard a fusillade of rifle fire followed by three single shots.

"Those bastards!" muttered Bob. "They really *are* using a plane to chase elk."

"What are you talking about?" asked Smitty.

Bob then angrily told Smitty of the conversation he'd overheard from the neighboring hunters the evening before, while the Cub circled twice and then cut its power to glide off toward the airport at Eagle.

"I ought to take a shot at the damned thing!" cried Bob.

"Well, one thing for sure: they found the herd we were trailing, and if we're going to make it back to camp by dark we'd better get going," Smitty said.

They retraced their steps to the ridge that Smitty had climbed the day before. By the time they reached the bottom there was so little daylight left that they almost walked past the power line that led back to camp.

Coming into the camp they noticed only one of the other party, and he, upon noticing Bob and Smitty, went into the trailer. Tired and disgusted, Smitty and Bob each downed a couple beers as they prepared their supper. About halfway through their meal they heard the other three hunters come whooping into camp.

"We did it, we really got 'em!" one of them shouted to the other hunter, who then stuck his head outside the trailer and asked, "How many?"

"Three!" boasted the first. "Bill got two and I got one. Hey, let's build another fire and really whoop it up tonight. Hey, Joe, bring my bottle of Jack Daniel's out with you and throw away the stopper. We're gonna celebrate!"

Bill, who was looking for a larger audience for the recitation of his great deeds, sauntered over to Bob's camper and offered a loud invitation to join the party.

Smitty replied, "As soon as we finish eating we'll be over, okay?"

"I'd choke to death drinking those rotten bastards' rotten whiskey!" mumbled Bob.

"Bob, as usual you're only partly right. Jack Daniel's is not rotten whiskey. It's so smooth no one could choke on it. I'm going to take a big glass over there and listen to the bastards blow."

"Go ahead if you want to. I'll wash the dishes. Maybe I'll come over after a while. Right now I feel like I'd probably get into a fight if I went over there."

After a second cup of coffee, Smitty helped Bob clear the table, and then sauntered on over to the other camp where the mighty hunters were jubilantly passing the bottle around their victory bonfire.

"So, how'd it go?" asked Smitty as he approached the rowdy group, brightly illuminated by the dancing flames.

"Terrific!" cried the exhilarated owner of the bottle. "Here, have a belt before this bottle is—hey, it's almost gone! Someone open up another! Bill over there got two, and I got one!"

"Bill over there," who'd shot two, was content to bask in drunken glory as "I got one" recounted the hunt.

The story, as it emerged, was that Joe had been sick and stayed in camp, while good-old Bill, who could practically smell elk, had led them straight up a ridge and right into a big herd. Bill, wise in the way of elk, immediately shot the lead cow, and then, while the herd was milling about in confusion, downed a yearling bull, while the owner of the bottle shot another cow.

The third hunter had a different lie to tell. He claimed to have seen a huge old bull elk and a young cow, and was just waiting for the bull to step out from behind a tree, when Bill started shooting. The bull whirled around and bolted back up the ridge and out of sight without his even being able to get off a shot. The truth, known only to the participants, was that the herd had again been pushed down the ridge by the plane, and had practically all regrouped, except for a young cow that Harold feared was about to escape from his harem. In his anxiety to recapture his wayward love, Harold had bumbled into the windy hunter. One glimpse of Harold's mighty antlers had given the lying hunter such a trembling case of buck fever that he couldn't even fumble his rifle off safety. He had frightened the bull off by his own ineptitude. He recited his tale with great bravado, however, ending it by saying that it was too bad the shooting had frightened the elk away, as he'd surely have shot two more and could have given Smitty and Bob the young cow.

Smitty laughed and replied that they wouldn't have been able to accept anything but the big old bull, as their non-resident licenses entitled them to possess only antlered elk.

The conversation then turned to how Bill was going to go back into Eagle the next day to rent a couple of pack horses to get the elk back down the ridge, while the others were to start clearing a trail over which the horses could be led up the mountainside.

Smitty noticed that Bob was still in their camper, probably too angry to come over and talk, so he excused himself and went back to turn in for the night.

"You were right about their using a plane," said Smitty once back in the camper. "I found out that the guy who supposedly stayed in camp all day is a flight instructor back in Denver."

"What a bunch of crumbs!" mumbled Bob from the warmth of his sleeping bag.

"I don't know about you, yawned Smitty, "but I've been up to the top of that darned mountain twice in two days, and I don't think I have energy enough to do it again. We're supposed to go to the Radsons' tomorrow for supper, so I think I'll just go up to that slide meadow and let it go at that. Those guys said that the elk all ran back up the mountain after the shooting, so Lord only knows where we might find them."

"Yeah, I guess we'll just have to play it by ear. Four hours to climb up to the timberline and three to get back down again sure doesn't leave much time for hunting. Maybe Jim will have an idea tomorrow night," said Bob just before falling asleep.

CHAPTER 10

Dawn of the third day found Smitty and Bob still in bed. The exertion of the previous two days' hunting, their lack of success, and their encounter with the other group of hunters had been fatiguing both physically and mentally.

Upon finally arising and enjoying a more leisurely breakfast, they decided to climb only partway up the mountain and to return to camp by four P.M. in order to arrive at the Radsons' for supper. Bob decided to try a ridge that lay just to the west of the camp, while Smitty, who'd lost almost all hope of shooting an elk, decided just to return to Maude's meadow and spend the day there. By the time they left camp, the sun had risen above the surrounding mountains and was again warming the valley unseasonably.

At eleven-thirty Smitty was looking for fresh tracks in the trail leading across the shale slide toward the meadow. Finding nothing, he edged carefully across the shale trail as quietly as possible, then followed the trail on through the dense dry spruce leading to the meadow. Arriving at its edge, he was not surprised to find it empty. Skirting down and around the meadow, Smitty paused on the berm-bench to eat the sandwich he'd stuffed into his pack earlier, and to feast on the view of the surrounding mountains, the valley below, its reservoir, and the CR Ranch farther down. The ranch was barely discernible to Smitty's naked eye, but, viewing it through his binoculars, he could make out not only the buildings but also a cattle truck backed up to the loading chute at the corral.

"Jim is shipping his calves today," he observed.

Sitting out in the open, enjoying both the sun and the view, Smitty's presence was soon noted by a sharp-eyed jaybird, who promptly started scolding from a nearby tree.

Well, old Mr. Jay, you and your big mouth are not about to let me ambush some poor unsuspecting elk, are you? thought Smitty wryly. *Guess I'll just poke around the edges of this meadow for the lack of anything better to do.*

At the south edge of the clearing, where the other trail entered, Smitty failed to find any fresh tracks leading either in or out of the meadow, so he proceeded up to the spring at the top of the clearing. Loitering around the nearly dry spring, he noticed how the elk had pawed the earth to form depressions in which water had collected. Seated on the grass nearby, and studying the steep bank of earth that remained above the spring after the hillside had slid away, he noticed some dead tree roots, which resembled bleached bones, protruding from the top of the bank. Approximately halfway up, perhaps twenty feet, something caught his eye. What had first appeared to be roots now looked like a partial skeleton of some animal. His curiosity aroused, Smitty laid aside his rifle and hunting gear, and scrambled up the bank for a closer look.

It was a skeleton, all right, but when he touched the exposed ribs they crumbled into dust. At first Smitty thought he'd discovered the remains of a sheep, but the shape of the skull puzzled him. It was horse-like in appearance and had flat front teeth, both uppers and lowers. Using the tip of his hunting knife he began to scrape away the earth covering the leg bones and discovered that the hoof was not cloven like that of a sheep, but was a distinctly single horse-like hoof.

A horse the size of a sheep? This must be some sort of old fossil. Still puzzled, he slid back down the bank to the spring to mull things over a bit.

What Smitty had discovered was the remains of a pliohippus, the one-toed forerunner of the modern horse. The spring, which was barely flowing at the time of Smitty's visit, had flowed much more profusely some 3 million years before. In the late tertiary period of the Cenozoic era, even as the Rocky Mountains were still rising, it had fed a quagmire into which Smitty's old "sheep-horse" had fallen and died. Heavy erosion shortly after the demise of the pliohippus had quickly covered the body with successive layers of sand and silt, thus partially fossilizing his remains.

The pliohippus even had a companion in death, whom Smitty might have noticed had he examined the area more carefully. What he had taken for a loose white rock close by the remains of pliohippus was in reality the broken tip of a mastodon tusk. The mastodon had fallen into the quagmire about a week before the pliohippus, and in the natural order of death he had first fought, trumpeting with rage, and then with fear, but had succeeded only in becoming more hopelessly mired. By the time the pliohippus ambled onto the scene, the mastodon had long since ceased his plaintive bleating, and, with the complete disinterested eyes of the near dead, watched the pliohippus slip and fall into the same trap. Struggling feebly and silently, lacking the stamina of the mastodon, the pliohippus died an hour before the mastodon on the following day. Perhaps each was grateful for the companionship of the other. More than likely, they became less and less aware of the other's presence, as each faced the awesome realization that one's last task here on earth must be performed alone!

When I get back home I'll have to go to the library and see if I can find out what sort of animal that was buried up there, thought Smitty. *Well, I'm sure not going to climb any farther up this durned mountain today. We're supposed to be back at the Radsons' for supper, so I might just as well go over there on the north side of the meadow and just sit in the sun for awhile.*

Skirting the north edge of the meadow, he found a perfect place about halfway down, with a commanding view of the spring at the upper end, the berm at the lower end, and both approaches to the meadow. By now the sun was past it zenith, and Smitty, reclining against a fallen log, promptly fell asleep in the near-eighty-degree heat. After sleeping perhaps an hour, something aroused him. Without moving, he scanned the meadow, but to no avail. Faint rustlings focused his attention on the south trail entrance. Another five minutes passed and then he caught sight of Old Maude standing in the middle of the south trail leading into the meadow, Charles at her flank.

That sly old beggar. She's as cautious as a wild deer, thought Smitty as he continued to bask in the pleasant warmth of the September sun.

Maude, exercising her usual care, stood semi-concealed a full ten minutes before she was satisfied as to the safety of the meadow. Once assured, she boldly sallied forth toward the spring, and Charles pranced out ahead of her.

This must be the only place to get water for quite some distance, reasoned Smitty as he glanced at his watch. *Well, it looks like it's time to go, so I'll just pack up and get on down the mountain early. That old cow must like this place as much as I do, so I'll just sneak out of here and leave them alone.* Picking up his gear, he slipped quietly away, shouldering neither rifle nor pack until he was out of the meadow and back into the woods.

Arriving back in camp early, Smitty found no one except Bill, the great hunter of the other party, who'd just returned from Eagle with a couple of packhorses and a rented horse trailer. His companions were still up the mountain clearing the trail for the horses. Bob Bine was also somewhere up there.

"Hey, you're just the guy I'm looking for," said Bill.

"How's that?" replied Smitty.

"I need someone to go fishing with me, that's what. The trout are running up this stream from the reservoir and I need some help," said Bill as he finished putting his rod together.

"That's a new one. I never heard of anyone needing help to catch a trout. I don't have a fishing license, but I suppose I could go along and watch."

"Come on, I'll get some trout for you guys too," said Bill as he finished rigging his fishing rod.

On the way down to the stream Bill explained that the fish they were after were really not trout but Konakee salmon, which had been stocked in the reservoir by the Colorado Department of Game and Fish. Every fall the salmon would attempt to spawn by running up the creek. Since they were spawning, they wouldn't bite on any bait offered. The fishing pole was just for show in case any game wardens were watching. Once they were down by the creek and concealed by the tag alders along its banks, Bill tossed his pole aside and began building a wing dam of rocks across a riffle just below a fair-sized fishing hole.

"Here now, you hold this dip net in the opening in the dam that I've left, and I'll go up around the bend and stir the hole up good with a stick," instructed Bill.

"Like hell I will!" replied Smitty. "This sounds like a snipe hunt. I'll be standing here like a damned fool holding that durned little net and you'll disappear. Back home they leave you holding a bag open at the end of a corn row, while they supposedly go off to chase the snipe down the row and into the bag. I'm dumb, but not stupid."

"Oh, hell, I'll hold the net then. You stir that hole up good, from the far end clear back on down to here."

Smitty did as he was told, and, as he came stirring his way around the bend, he saw Bill busy scooping salmon onto the bank, four or five fish per dip. By the time Smitty reached the lower end of the pool, Bill had thirty-six fat salmon flopping about on the bank.

"It's all very easy if you know how," grinned Bill smugly. "Is a half dozen enough for your supper, or should we try another hole?"

"We're heading out of here this afternoon, and we're supposed to go down to the CR Ranch for supper with Bob's cousin. Some other time, maybe."

"Aw, take some anyway. You've got a cooler in that camper, haven't you?" Bill said, kicking his wing dam apart.

"Well, we spent a hundred and fifty bucks for elk licenses, and it doesn't look to me as though we're going to get anything. I suppose a few fish won't hurt much," replied Smitty.

Upon Bob's return, Smitty was back in the camper, his face flushed by a few swigs from Bill's bottle of bourbon, and his ill-gotten salmon cleaned and concealed in the refrigerator.

After having heard Smitty's fish story and viewed the salmon lying on ice, Bob said, "For crissake! Those damned slobs can't even fish honest. I feel like going over there and smacking that bastard right in the mouth!"

"You know I had a part in it too. But you're right, they *are* a bunch of slobs."

"Well," glowered Bob, "it just makes me madder than hell! Using a plane to hunt elk and a net to catch fish!"

"Bob, my old grandpa had a saying about that sort of people. He used to say, 'You can't stop turds from stinking by kicking them around.' They probably do stink, but their good bourbon sure doesn't. Come on, let's get on down to the Radsons' and see what tomorrow will bring."

CHAPTER 11

Arriving back at the CR Ranch only slightly early for supper, Bob Bine noticed the absence of most of the young stock and commented, "Jim must have sold his calves."

Smitty replied, "Yesterday afternoon I was up at that slide meadow, and I could see a couple big livestock trucks through my binoculars. I forgot to tell you about it last night."

"Maybe he'll be able to get us up above the timberline early enough to get in a little hunting. Riding a horse up that mountain can't be much harder than hiking up," Bob said as they drove up to the house.

Radson and his sons were waiting at the door to greet the hunters. As a preliminary, Jim inquired about their hunting. "Any luck?"

"Nothing," said Bob rather tersely.

"Nothing? I sure can't understand that; I saw elk practically every time I was up there last summer. Well, come on in. Sue's got everything almost ready, so you can tell your hard-luck story at the table."

Sue's table, laden with produce from her garden and a large roast of beef, so whetted Smitty's appetite that he was content to stuff himself while letting Bob tell the tale. During the course of the meal, Bob related their three-day hunt from beginning to end. When he came to the parts concerning the hunters with the airplane and radios, he became so agitated that he almost quit eating.

Jim then replied, "Using an airplane was surely illegal, but if you want to turn them in to the Fish and Game Department, both of you would have to return to Colorado to testify against them. I can't keep them off our leased land, but if I ever catch them on CR property I'll run them off."

Throughout most of the meal Bob had become so engrossed in relating the happenings of the previous three days that he failed to realize he'd fallen behind—everyone else was waiting for him to finish eating so Sue could serve dessert and coffee. Finally noticing what he'd done, he rather sheepishly said, "Smitty is the one who should be telling this. He's the one who saw all the elk. All I saw was an old Hereford cow and her calf, and they about scared me half to death."

Returning to the conversation, Smitty told the Radsons that Bob had correctly related the unfortunate hunting trip, and how they'd seen the old cow and her calf on each of the preceding days.

"That's your Old Maude and her blamed red calf," said Jim to Sue. "We didn't catch her in the roundup this fall."

At this, Sue explained to Bob and Smitty how Maude had come to be named, and how she had fought Jim off from her calf at birth and had managed to slip off up the mountain with it.

"I'll bet I know just where she is right now," Smitty ventured. "There's a meadow up there on the side of the mountain. I saw her up there every day since we got there last Friday. As a matter of fact, the elk were there on the first day also, but your Old Maude spooked them out before I could get a shot. That meadow is one of the most pleasant places I've ever been. It has sort of a bench on the bottom that you can stand on and see over the treetops clear down here to the bottom of the valley. From down here the trees hide the meadow, but on top of the bench you can see the ranch. It has a small spring too, but it's almost dry right now. Say, that reminds me of something I saw up there this afternoon.

I guess I even forgot to tell Bob about it. Right above the spring there's a dirt bank and there's some animal's bones sticking out. I think it's some sort of fossil because I've never seen anything like it before. They look like horse bones, but the whole skeleton is only as big as a sheep. It has to be a fossil."

Just then the younger of the two Radson boys, seizing upon an opportunity to skip school and go hunting, interrupted: "Dad, maybe we'd better stay home tomorrow and go along with you guys to get Old Maude down off the mountain before the snow comes."

"Oh, no you don't! You and your brother are going to school as usual, and as soon as you finish your dessert you'd better get to your lessons." Then softening somewhat, Jim said, "If we manage to get them down, you guys can have the calf to raise and sell."

"I don't think it would be too hard to drive them down," said Smitty. "If one of us came down the south ridge and chased them out of the meadow onto the north ridge, a couple guys could keep them from going back up the mountain and then the three of us could drive them on down that same ridge. It has a pretty good game trail, and it comes out right by the southwest corner of your pasture."

"I hiked up that trail last spring, but I sure can't remember any meadow," said Jim.

"You can't see it from either ridge," replied Smitty. "There's just a faint trail forking off some hard rock to the south, then it crosses a shale slide into some thick spruce. The meadow is on the other side of the spruce."

"Some trail," scoffed Bob. "You wouldn't catch me trying to get a horse down those ridges and across that shale."

"We'd have to walk," Smitty said.

"Let's see," mused Jim. "It would take three of us to drive them out of the meadow and down the ridge leading to the pasture, and someone would have to bring the horses back down and open up the fence over by the creek."

"Why not let the boys go along?" asked Sue. "One day out of school isn't all that bad, and besides, what if it should start snowing like it did last fall? Old Maude and her calf would probably be trapped up there and die."

"Well, I suppose missing one day wouldn't hurt them too much, and I sure would hate to lose any stock up there in the snow. All right, boys, help your mom clear the table and then bring your books in here. We'll take our coffee out in the living room and talk about the hunting for tomorrow. You kids will have to get up extra early, so I want you in bed extra early too."

Proceeding into the living room, Jim added another log to the fireplace, commenting that the evenings were still pretty chilly despite the unusually warm fall. "By this time last fall there was three feet of snow on top of the mountain. This weather could break anytime, although tomorrow's forecast is for continued unseasonably warm."

"Well, now," continued Jim, "tomorrow we'll take all four of our horses. The two boys can ride double. We'll leave just before daylight.

"Smitty and I don't know much about horses, Jim," worried Bob.

"I have a couple gentle old mares for you. Got 'em for the boys to learn on. All you have to do is to hang on to the saddle's pommel and up we'll go up easy as pie. You could almost drive a jeep up that trail. About two and a half hours will put us up top."

"We'll manage somehow," said Smitty with a wink. "Sure sounds better than five hours hiking up the ridge on foot."

"I fed the cattle a double ration this evening so I won't have to do chores in the morning. We'll saddle up about a half hour before dawn, so that means breakfast at five. By the way, Sue is planning to fix breakfast and pack a lunch for us to take along. I can't guarantee that you'll see elk tomorrow, as I've never hunted them myself. I did see plenty of them up there all last summer, but, if they've been shot at like you said, they could be anywhere. If we can't locate any by two o'clock, chances are they'll be holed up in some heavy timber down along some ridge."

"That's fair enough," said Smitty. "After two o'clock, Bob can go down the back ridge and chase Old Maude out of her meadow. I'll take both of the boys with me down the front ridge and keep them from going back up. Bob, do you think you could find the back way into the meadow again?"

"Hey, if I could find my way up from that meadow, I sure could find my way back!"

"Okay, then you get to shag them out. We'll keep them from going back up, and then all four of us will herd them on down. In the meantime Jim can bring the horses down and open up the pasture fence."

"I don't know about you two," exclaimed Bob, "but if I have to ride a durned horse up the side of a mountain in the dark, I'm going to go to bed early—and say my prayers."

"I expect it would be wise to turn in early," said Jim. "Tomorrow is going to be a long day."

Just then Sue and the boys emerged from the kitchen, dishes and homework finished. Jim saw the boys off to bed and returned to the living room, where he found Bob and Sue deep in conversation about mutual relatives back in Iowa. Having not been very well acquainted with Sue's family, Jim allowed Smitty to draw him into a separate discussion about ranching. Without realizing it, Jim Radson, in response to Smitty's questioning, spoke of all his hopes, his plans, and the financial condition of the CR.

The ranch was not making any money as yet, due partly to the cattle cycle and partly to the poor quality of the CR cattle. Nationwide, cattle numbers had peaked two years earlier and had depressed prices, but Jim felt that now was the time to break into the business. With his friend and partner, John Colvin, providing the capital, Jim hoped to upgrade the herd, and when the cycle brought an upswing in prices, they'd be sitting pretty.

Shortly before ten P.M., somewhat to Smitty's relief, Sue rescued him from Jim, who'd become so involved explaining the breeding of cattle, that he'd even brought out the papers of his most prized possession, Black Hercules.

"Jim, Smitty's not interested in that bull's bloodline. These fellows are out here to go hunting. Besides, it wouldn't hurt you to think of something besides cattle now and then. Tomorrow you'd better get us some elk meat for the table. I'm getting tired of beef all the time."

"Shucks!" Jim responded. "They tell me elk tastes just like beef."

"Yuck!" exclaimed Sue. "Maybe you can find a pig up there and shoot it. I'm hungry for some pork chops."

"Yuck again!" cried Bob. "Now you've ruined my vacation by reminding me of my crummy job. Pork chops! Smitty and I slice off thousands and thousands of them every day! I'm going to bed. Tomorrow I have to ride a horse for the first time since I was a little kid riding a pony at the county fair. Good night to all of you."

CHAPTER 12

The Radson boys had slept dreaming of the forthcoming hunt, and, when aroused by Jim, dressed quickly, gulped their breakfast, and dashed outside to saddle the mounts. By the time the men emerged from the house, the horses were waiting beneath the yard light.

Disdainfully gesturing over his shoulder with his thumb toward two rather large quarter-horse mares, the youngest Radson said to Bob and Smitty, "Dad says you two get old Nell and Bell."

Both boys had long since grown tired of the proffered mounts' lumbering gaits, and now considered Nell and Bell fit only to be harnessed to the bobsled used for hauling hay to the cattle throughout the winter.

As he strapped his rifle scabbard onto his saddle, Jim said, "You fellows will have to ride with your rifles slung across your backs. Don't worry about those old nags, they're gentle as kittens. Just don't shoot from the saddle—I'd expect they couldn't take that and might become something else."

A closer examination of Nell and Bell, standing solidly out in the yard with their reins dangling onto the ground, convinced the two dudes that there probably was not much to fear.

As Bob awkwardly climbed onto his horse, Jim laughed and said, "Just relax and let Bell do all the work."

"Dad, can we lead?" asked Jimmy, the elder of the boys.

"No. I want you and Donnie in the back all day long, not dashing

64

out in front spooking all the game. I'll lead, Bob and Smitty next, and you two in the rear. Keep quiet and keep out of the lunch in those saddlebags—that's for all of us, not just for you boys."

With a wink and a wave to Sue, who was standing in the open doorway, Jim wheeled his mount and led the hunting party up the mountain. Approximately halfway up he halted the group to rest the horses. Much to Smitty's relief, the trail was, as Jim had claimed, an easy one. Even though he knew he'd have sore muscles later on, he was still grateful not to be ascending the mountain afoot. By eight-thirty they had completed the second leg and had arrived at the timberline.

Once there, Jim laid out his strategy for the hunt. He decided to split the group by sending Bob and Smitty around the timberline's eastern slopes. The Radsons were to poke about down in the scrub timber below them. Smitty and Bob, with their scope-sighted rifles, were to stay out in the clear. They would hunt on horseback and meet about noon somewhere on the northern slope. It was an excellent strategy, but the heat, and the pressure of being hunted, had caused the elk to bed down in the shade on a cool, spruce-covered slope. Shortly after noon the two groups had rejoined and dismounted for lunch.

"I can't believe this heat," said Bob, noting that everyone had stripped down to shirtsleeves "Did you see anything, Jim? We didn't."

"Not a thing. You can bet all the elk are holed up someplace nice and cool."

"A year ago there was at least three feet of snow up here. I've been here in July and found it cooler than now," Jim mused.

"We might as well eat and then go and get that cow and calf back home. There's sure as heck no elk up here anymore," said Bob.

After finishing their lunch, they cut across the flat mountaintop and dropped Bob off at the south ridge leading down to the slide meadow. Bob's old Bell then became Donnie's mount, for which the boy was grateful after having had to ride double all morning. They then rode over to the north ridge, where Smitty gave his mount over to Jim, who said, "Take it nice and slow. I'll need almost four hours to get down and open up the pasture fence."

Bob Bine, who was a pretty fair woodsman, had no trouble finding his way down the ridge or finding the trail leading over to the meadow, which he followed as quietly as possible. Even so, Maude, who had been lying on top of the berm at the lower end of the meadow, was aware of his presence long before he emerged into the clearing. She let Bob get almost halfway across the opening and then jumped up and bolted toward the trail from which Bob had just emerged, with Charles running at her heels. Seeing that Maude was making for the trail behind him, Bob wheeled and ran back toward the trail, shouting to head her off. When Maude saw her escape route cut off, she stopped and then began herding Charles toward the other trail leading out of the meadow. Just as she disappeared into the woods, Bob shouted, then fired a shot into the air to keep her moving. Then he ran across the meadow and down the trail to crowd them across the slide. Charles, who'd grown quite nimble during the summer, scrambled across the slippery trail like a goat; but Maude, moving more slowly, was less than halfway when Bob caught up. Seeing her ahead, Bob let out another loud whoop. Maude redoubled her efforts, lost her footing, and tumbled down the shale slide in an avalanche of rock. Landing across a dead tree at the bottom of the slide, she broke her back.

Ten minutes later Smitty and Jimmy arrived on the scene to find Charles on their side of the slide, looking down at his mother in consternation.

"What happened?" shouted Smitty.

"That old cow fell and slid down to the bottom," Bob called back. "Looks like she's hurt bad."

"Jimmy, you and Donnie chase that calf down the ridge a bit so he can't get back up past us," said Smitty. "Bob, can you get down to her from over there?"

"God, I don't know," Bob shouted back. "I don't think I'd better try or I'll wind up like her."

"Can you get over here?" called Smitty, noting that Jimmy had been successful in herding the frightened calf down the ridge. "I don't think I ought to try to get down there either."

"I think I can get across to your side," replied Bob, who by now realized that he was responsible for Maude's plight. Twice while Bob crept across the slide trail, Old Maude got up onto her front legs, but fell back bellowing in pain. When Bob finally reached Smitty, he was shaking violently and had to sit down, By this time Jimmy had returned to the scene.

"What do you think, Jimmy? We couldn't get her out of there even if she could walk, and I don't think we could get down there to butcher her without a rope," said Smitty.

"That skinny old cow wouldn't even make good hamburger," said Jimmy, "and the market ain't any good anyhow. You'd better just shoot her."

Without another word Smitty unslung his rifle and sighted it onto a spot just between and slightly above Maude's unblinking eyes. The rifle slammed into his shoulder, and Maude sighed and slumped back onto her side almost peacefully. Smitty, without visibly showing it, was dismayed. He had killed animals before without remorse; this was the first time he had ever done so as an act of kindness.

As the trio proceeded down the ridge with the balky Charles before them, Smitty ruefully thought, *Some hunter I am: I go after the noble elk and wind up killing a poor old Hereford cow!*

It was four o'clock when they reached Jim and the pasture fence. They managed to get the somewhat subdued Charles across the fence that Jim had taken down, and then started to drive him across the pasture to a holding pen near the barn.

When told of the incident, Jim said, "She wasn't worth much on the market, and I was going to cull her anyhow. Well, there's no need to put this fence back up right now, so let's chase this red bugger on up to the barn. Might as well trim and brand him tonight. That ought to take some of the sass out of him. Donnie, ride on up to the barn and plug in the branding iron. I'll fix him up as soon as we get him up there."

Charles turned out to be an unruly handful. He tried everything possible to escape, but was eventually driven into the corral and from there into the squeeze chute that Jim used to treat cattle. Rather than rope and tie them for castration and branding as the old-timers did, he had built a squeeze chute, copying it from pictures in his stockman's periodical. It worked well on larger cattle, but the stanchion clamping the animals' necks didn't really close tight enough for calves.

"Dad, the iron is red-hot already," said Donnie.

"Well, go ahead and brand him, then."

The youngest Radson unplugged the iron and reached through the chute, pressing it too high on the flank. The top of the "R" on the CR branding iron projected above Charles's hipbone. When the iron struck, Charles reared, bawling in pain, and the brand was botched. Once the burn healed, the brand would read "Ch"—the diminutive abbreviation of Charles—rather than CR, an error or coincidence that Sue Radson would eventually notice and use. As if botching up the brand weren't bad enough, Donnie also managed to drop the iron onto the floor of the chute where Charles's flying hooves quickly broke it.

"You damned red calf!" cursed Jim after retrieving the iron. "I'll make a steer out of you now!" he cried, seizing the Burdizzo clamp. An instrument invented by an Italian veterinarian, it resembles a pair of large pincers, and uses its compound leverage to crush the spermatic cord connecting the testicle to the body without severing the scrotum. The clamp is applied twice, once above each testicle.

Jim crawled over the chute, knelt behind Charles, and applied the clamp above the left testicle. Charles bellowed in pain and managed to tear loose from the stanchion holding his head. In the fracas following, Jim wrenched his bad back and fell beneath Charles. When Smitty quickly opened the chute to rescue Jim, Charles charged wildly out, ran through an open gate, across the pasture and over the fence that Jim had taken down, and into the woods and freedom.

Jim was in great pain while Bob, Smitty, and the boys assisted him to the house. Once there, Sue managed to get Jim settled into bed with his heating pad, while Bob and Smitty went out to help the boys with the evening chores.

"What a day!" groaned Bob as he crawled into his bunk in the pickup camper that night. "My legs and fanny hurt me as much as Jim's back must hurt him. That darned old mare just about did me in! To hell with hunting tomorrow! I'm going to sleep in. At least you got to shoot something. I didn't."

Yeah, I know," replied Smitty as he zipped his sleeping bag shut. When he closed his eyes he couldn't avoid the picture of old Maude lying at the bottom of the ravine. Sleep came slowly to Smitty that night.

CHAPTER 13

On Wednesday, the fifth day of their hunt, Smitty and Bob were rudely awakened at five-thirty by Jimmy's pounding on the door of their camper.

"Mom says to come on in for breakfast, and Dad wants to see you. He's still in bed with his sore back."

"Cripes, are my legs ever sore!" complained Bob, attempting to climb out of his bunk. "It was that big fat old mare! Ow! oh, Ow, Ow! I don't think I'll be able to walk from here over to the Radsons' house."

"Okay, you stay here and fix your own breakfast, then. I'd crawl over there before I'd eat your bacon and eggs again," Smitty joked. "I'm sore too. I couldn't walk or ride up that mountain again today no matter what."

"The weather and everything else just seems to be against us," groaned Bob. "What say we go home?"

"Might as well," replied Smitty, "but we don't have to be back until Sunday. How about a little sightseeing on the way home? We bored holes in the dark all the way out here. Let's detour up through Wyoming and the Black Hills. I've never seen any of that country before."

Once in the ranch house they went directly into the bedroom and found Jim propped up in bed, a cup of coffee in his hands. "If you want to," Jim said, "you can take the horses up by yourselves. As you can see, I won't be doing anything for a couple days. The boys will do the chores this morning, and then Sue can drive them to school later on."

No way!" replied Bob. We decided to give it up for this year. The weather, our rotten luck, and my aching muscles are all against us. The only way I could get up that mountain today would be for someone to carry me up on a stretcher. We've decided to head on home today."

"We'll do your chores," said Smitty. "There's no need for the boys to miss any more school. Just tell us what needs to be done. How about tomorrow and the next couple days?"

"Well, if you don't mind, you could fill up all the feeders with hay. That would probably last until Saturday morning. By then I'll be better and the boys will be home from school for the weekend. Sure was too bad that I couldn't get you up to see some elk. There are a few around, all right, but you're right about the weather. They'll be hard to find until the snow forces them down. Come back again next year and things will probably be different. Say! I smell hotcakes. You'd better get yourselves out into the kitchen. My wife feeds all the working hands first. I'm getting hungry, but I'm no longer a working hand."

Just then, Sue entered the room with a tray, and announced that Bob and Smitty had best get into the kitchen, as the boys were already eating and probably would shortly gobble down everything in sight.

The youngest Radson boy, seeing Bob ease himself gently onto his chair at the kitchen table, said, "Old Nell sure got to you, didn't she?"

"Man, I sure am stiff from galloping up and down that mountain," replied Bob.

"Old Nell doesn't gallop, she just plods along like a plow horse. You'd have to pound a stake into the ground alongside of her just to see if she were moving."

"Just for that, young fellow, Smitty and I are going to do your chores for you and you'll have to go to school as usual."

"Say, I can't wait to get there and tell all the other guys about these two dudes who came out here elk hunting and shot one of our cows."

"Smitty, I really think he's actually going to tattle on us. We'd better go on home before all the kids here in Eagle start laughing at us," said Bob as he heaped his plate with food.

Having finished Sue's breakfast, the two hunters bid farewell to the two young Radsons at the school-bus door, and then began feeding the cattle. Rather than attempt to harness Nell and Bell to the wagon, something the two neophytes hadn't the vaguest idea how to do, they used the tractor to pull the wagon loaded with bales of hay from the stack to the feed bunks.

Meanwhile, a very short distance up the mountain, Charles was stoically enduring the results of his treatment by his only human acquaintances. The brand on his flank burned fiercely, but was nothing compared to the pain between his hind legs. Licking the brand seemed to ease that pain somewhat, but any attempt to walk or even to stand caused him great torment. It would take him another whole day to reach the slide meadow to rest and quench his thirst at the spring.

While at the pen of cattle containing the prized bull, Black Hercules, Smitty commented to Bob that for a bull Hercules wasn't very aggressive. He allowed most of the CR cows to crowd him away from the feeder.

Doing the chores and packing the camper for the trip home consumed most of the morning, and, as usual, Sue invited them for the noon meal. On this occasion the two greenhorns managed to contribute more than big appetites: Smitty brought his ill-gotten salmon in to share with the Radsons.

It was almost two P.M. before they finally managed to be on their way. Six-thirty found them just on the outskirts of Denver, where they found a trailer campground for the night.

CHAPTER 14

Having left the CR Ranch late Wednesday, Bob and Smitty traveled at a more leisurely rate on their way home. Late Thursday morning found them at the Mount Rushmore Memorial in the Black Hills of South Dakota.

Upon viewing the gigantic faces carved from the mountainside, Bob Bine, with his imperfect knowledge of history, said, "That's really neat the way they're all lined up from left to right, just like they followed each other in history."

Smitty thought, "Oh great! Washington, Jefferson, Roosevelt, and Lincoln all in order?" Smitty said, "Yup, pretty neat all right, Bob."

One of their other bits of sightseeing, while driving through the Black Hills, was a tour of Jewel Cave, which Smitty found depressing, commenting that it reminded him of the windowless plant where they worked. "I feel buried in both places."

Bob, in reply, managed a rather profound (for him) observation: "Maybe, but where else could we earn a living that pays as well without a college degree?"

Refueling in Rapid City, with a late lunch at a fast-food restaurant, they decided to get off the freeway and travel secondary roads to Pierre, South Dakota, hoping to see a few antelope, which they did, sighting several herds of antelope and numerous mule deer.

Arriving at Pierre late that evening, they crossed the Missouri

River just above the city on a road atop a mammoth earthen dam holding back miles of impounded water in the Oahe Reservoir. Both thought that a tour of the dam's powerhouse and generators would be interesting, and, since they'd missed the last tour of the day, they decided to stay over and make the first tour of the next day.

While driving south from the dam to Pierre, Smitty said, "I feel more than a little grubby after two nights of camping out. Why don't we get a motel, shower, and then eat out tonight?"

Bob agreed, and after a bit of shopping they found an inexpensive but clean motel in downtown Pierre. "Where's a good place to eat?" Bob asked the owner while they were registering.

"Most everyone here goes to the D&E down on Missouri Street. It's only four blocks from here; good everyday food," was the reply.

Sure enough, on Missouri Street they found a small cafe, a hole in the wall with a neon sign above the door: D&E Cafe, Open 24 hr./day, 7 days/week.

"Well, why not?" said Smitty. "It comes highly recommended."

Surprise of surprises, the steaks they ordered came complete with soup, salad, and dessert, and were of good quality. Upon finishing the meal and complimenting the waitress for both food and service, Bob asked, "Where's my bill? You only gave us one.

The waitress said, "The bill is for both of you. If you want to pay separately just divide it in two." Then she left them sitting there, mouths agape.

"Two steak dinners for only six dollars and fifty cents? That's only three and a quarter apiece! And with dessert too!" gasped Bob.

After leaving a healthy tip and while settling up with the D&E manager, Bob asked, "What's there to do around here evenings?"

"Well, most people go across the river to Fort Pierre," said the manager. "They're on Rocky Mountain Time and don't close until two A.M. their time. Bars on this side of the river don't stand a chance. The Silver Spur over there has a band on Fridays and Saturdays. Lots of folks come in for the dancing. We get a lot of business mornings after they close up."

Upon stepping outside into the chilly night air, Smitty said, "Why not? I haven't had a drink since we were up in the mountains camping out with that bunch of game hogs, and they were sure lousy company. From the looks of those three commercial TV channels listed in the motel, most anything would be better than a night of watching that. Besides, it seems like all I ever do back home is watch the tube."

"Okay by me," said Bob. "Let's walk back to the motel, get the truck, and go check out that Silver Spur."

After re-crossing the river to Ft. Pierre over a bridge between the cities, Bob and Smitty were surprised at what they found inside the Silver Spur bar. People were dancing to Western music played by a band using no amplifiers. They found they could even talk to each other without having to shout over the blare of extra-loud music.

"I don't believe this! Back home you need earplugs to go to a bar," said Smitty. "Look, there's a couple empty stools on this end of the bar. We'd better grab them. I don't see anyplace else to sit."

"What'll you have?" asked the bartender.

"Beer, replied Bob.

"You got rye whiskey?" asked Smitty.

"Sure. What with?"

"Water."

"Comin' right up."

"I've never seen a bar like this anywhere," said Smitty to Bob. "Look at the crowd. Ranch cowboys and reservation Indians.

Hope to hell we don't get into trouble here."

"Better not," said the bartender as he returned with the drinks. "Nobody fights here, not even outside. Try it and you'll sure do a little time in jail. Two-fifty for the drinks.

"Cripes, I've never seen prices like this anywhere. I think I'll start stopping in here on my way home after work," said Bob.

"Pretty long drive. Your old lady would kill you for being late to supper every night."

"'Old lady?' Who's got an old lady? I feel like kicking up my heels and dancing," said Bob. "In case anyone asks tonight, I'm single. You've got a wife and eight kids!"

The two of them downed a couple of drinks while talking about their plans for the next day. Once they had purchased the third round, Bob commented that the booth across the room had two women and only one man. "That dark-haired gal against the wall seems to be alone. I think I'll go over there and see if I can get a dance."

One thing about Bob, he's sure got nerve, observed Smitty as he watched his pal making his pitch. Smitty had always had trouble meeting strangers, especially strangers of the opposite sex. As a matter of fact, his wife had been forced to approach him. While contemplating all that, and watching Bob waltz around the dance floor, Smitty became somewhat glum. He was startled to hear a soft voice asking, "What's the matter? Don't you dance?"

Looking around he noticed that the barstool on his right was now occupied by a round-faced and rather sturdy young woman who was obviously a Native American Sioux.

"Naw, I don't know how. Guess I don't have any sense of rhythm. At least that's what my wife tells me."

"Too bad," was the reply.

"I think so too," smiled Smitty without realizing that the alcohol was releasing some of his inhibitions. Noting that both his and her glasses were almost empty, he ordered another for both.

"Thanks," replied the pleasant voice.

"No problem. You from around here?"

"I live out east of here with my Ma. When I'm not here in town working."

"What do you do?"

"Right now I'm clerking in the dime store. I used to be a legal secretary up in Mobridge."

"Why'd you quit that?"

"Got married. Big mistake."

"Oh? Why's that?"

She smiled a gap-toothed smile and replied, "That's why!" she said pointing to the missing tooth. "Tooth's gone and so is the husband. Guess which one I miss the most?"

"That's a pretty good philosophy!" laughed Smitty.

Warming up to the conversation, Smitty asked, "Are you Sioux?"

"Part Mandan, part Sioux, and part French."

"French?"

"Yup. Ever hear of the Metis?"

"Oh sure, Louis Reil and the Metis revolution against the British up in the Red River Valley."

"That's us. I'm just a little bit French. My Dad was Metis, so, according to your custom, my maiden name would be DeLorme, LaVonne DeLorme. What's your name?"

"Smith."

"Ha! That's rich! John Smith, I suppose?"

No, actually it's Loren Smith—everyone calls me Smitty."

"Well, if you say so," LaVonne said, a twinkle in her eye.

"Aw, hell! It's the truth," Smitty said with disgust. "You know something? The Minnesota Chippewa used to come down from up North and kick the hell out of you Sioux just for the fun of it."

"You know something about history, don't you?"

"Oh, just a little bit," he replied.

LaVonne laughed and said, "Stay right here, I've got somebody I want you to meet. I'll be right back."

"Now what the hell?" wondered Smitty as LaVonne returned with a great huge fellow of obvious Native American heritage.

"Smitty, I want you to meet George Bearfoot. He's my cousin and he's mostly Ojibwa. Most of them are a lot bigger than the Sioux."

George wasn't very talkative, but did explain that he had come to Pierre from northern Minnesota to work as an ironworker on the Garrison and Oahe Dam projects. He liked the country and wanted to stay on, but found that decent-paying jobs were scarce in the area. In reply to LaVonne's kidding about his size, he claimed he got that way from having grown up on a balanced diet containing the carbohydrates found in wild rice, rather than existing solely on buffalo fat like the Sioux did. After exchanging a few more pleasantries, he went back to his friends.

"Their size didn't do them much good after you Sioux got horses and guns," Smitty observed. "Your tribe turned into a bunch of hellions after that, didn't they?"

"Yup, the Sioux were doing pretty good until you palefaces showed up on the scene. And by the way, I'm only partly Sioux. My Dad was French and Mandan."

"Sure crazy how things turned out," said Smitty.

"Not crazy, it's just the way things happened. Everyone had different values. We just wanted to live off the land; you palefaces wanted to own the land you lived on. Your ancestors wanted it for themselves, and they weren't willing to share it. I've even got a bit of that land-grabbing in me. Probably got it from my French ancestors. My Ma has one hundred and sixty acres of farming land that she inherited. Half of it's going to be mine someday, and I'm going to keep it. I'm not a reservation Sioux."

"That's interesting," observed Smitty.

"I'm not like that damned Mary that your buddy's dancing with. She's going to clean his pockets before the night's over! Just you wait and see."

"That's also interesting," observed Smitty looking at Bob across the dance floor. "I also see that we're out of booze. Bartender!"

It was becoming apparent to Smitty that he was talking to someone with a reasonable education and better-than-average reasoning. He also noticed the warmth radiating from her body.

"I went to college for two and a half years, and I was a legal secretary for three more. That damned Mary spent more time than that lying on her back. You better watch out for your pal."

"Okay, okay! I'll try. Why is it that all your ancestors had no interest in owning land and you seem to feel differently?"

"Evolution," was her reply. "If you want to survive in this changing world, you have to learn to change."

About that time Bob came over and said, " Hey, Smitty, I found us an empty booth. C'mon, bring your friend over and join us."

Feeling the necessity of watching over Bob, as LaVonne had warned him, and not wishing to end the conversation he was involved in, Smitty asked, "How about it, LaVonne? Want to come along?"

"No, but I will. Don't expect me to be nice, though."

Somewhat surprised that Smitty had taken an interest in the short, moon-faced woman sitting next to him, Bob gallantly escorted them both across the room and then marched up to the bar for another round of drinks. Once all were settled into the booth, the talk that evolved was anything but friendly. When Smitty, in an attempt at polite conversation, asked Mary what tribe she was of, Mary replied, "Lakota Sioux."

"Ha! Why didn't you mention Crow, Blackfoot, and Arikara too?" retorted LaVonne. "She's from the Standing Rock Reservation."

"That's not so. My Pa is John Greyhorse! I'm all Sioux."

"Oh, that is a smart woman. She knows her own father," snipped LaVonne. "She's straight off the reservation."

"You're just mad because the Lakota were braver than the Mandan. You know it was one of the Lakota braves that died up on the hill by the dam, and was honored with the turtle."

"What's the turtle about?" asked Bob.

"This guy, he was a Lakota Sioux, and he had fought bravely, and he'd been shot on the hill right next to where the dam is now. As he ran away, wherever a drop of his blood fell onto the ground, my people put a rock; and where he died they built a turtle out of stones."

"Hey, that sounds interesting," said Smitty. "We're going out to the dam tomorrow. Maybe we could look it up."

"You won't find it," said LaVonne.

"Why not?" asked Bob.

"Well, the stones aren't there anymore," said Mary.

"Why's that?" asked Smitty.

"Because Mary and her tribe stole them," replied LaVonne. "Go ahead and tell them what you did."

"Well, I just took two of them, but I still have them in my drawer at home," Mary stated.

"Big deal! You stole your own heritage! Ha!" laughed LaVonne.

About that time the band quit playing and started to pack away their instruments. The bar was about to close.

"Say, I'm hungry," Bob said. "What say we all go back across the river to Pierre and stop in at the D&E Cafe?"

"No." said LaVonne. "I live over here in Fort Pierre, and I don't need anything to eat. I'm already too darned fat."

"Well, then, could we give you a lift home?" asked Bob.

"No. I only live a block away. The night air will be good."

"Do you want me to walk you there?" asked Smitty.

"No. Good night. You take care of your pal like I told you, and by the way, Smitty, I enjoyed the evening. Thanks," concluded LaVonne as she got up and walked out into the night.

Bob, Mary, and Smitty then got into the truck and drove back across the bridge to Pierre. While in the bathroom at the D&E Cafe, Bob announced that he and Mary were going to shack up that night.

"Okay, if you think you must. I'll sleep out in the camper, but first give me all your credit cards and all of your cash except for fifty dollars."

"What the hell for?" asked Bob.

"Just shut up and do it!" said Smitty.

The following morning, at ten-thirty Central Time, Smitty was awakened by Bob's barging into the camper. "Smitty, for cripes sake, I've been had. I woke up a little while ago and found my billfold lying on the floor, empty. Thank God you took most of my cash and my credit cards. I didn't tell you that I had two fifty-dollar bills hidden in a secret compartment of that wallet. They're gone too. A hundred and fifty bucks! Oh, crap!"

"Ain't love wonderful?" groaned Smitty as he sat up and discovered that his head seemed about to burst. "Let me go shower, and then we'll go down to the D&E for some coffee and break-fast—and some serious talk about going on home."

THE RETURN

Chapter 15

November 1975 provided most unusual weather for the Colorado Rockies. It grew colder, temperatures dropping to the teens and below, but the usual winter snows refused to fall.

Ski resorts at Vail and Aspen, lacking snowmaking equipment, were forced to remain closed. The owners cried, "Hard times!"

Not so for Charles, high on the mountainside at his mother's meadow. Three days after his arrival there, he was able to move about with much less pain. The brand on his flank had scabbed over and was healing, and the pain in his scrotum had subsided. His left testicle was beginning to atrophy.

The grass of the meadow, while frozen and dead, contained nearly all the nutrients of hay, and the spring still flowed from the frozen ground. Charles's diet was sufficient to maintain his body weight.

That the ground itself was frozen was most unusual, for snow usually fell early enough in the season to form a protective and insulating blanket over the soil. The frozen earth of the mountain would cause considerable flooding in the valley below in the following spring. Snow came so late that the first measurable amount fell on the seventh of December, and that was only three inches in depth. Charles had no trouble eking out a living on the slide meadow until mid-December, when heavy snow finally arrived and forced him down into the valley.

The campground at the reservoir was open enough to have

grown a reasonable amount of grass, and the creek remained open wherever the water tumbled down a riffle.

As Christmas approached, Charles had consumed almost all of the available grass in the campground. The snow in the valley deepened, making even that scanty supply harder to obtain, so he started working his way down the valley alongside the creek. On the afternoon of Christmas Eve, Charles ran into the fence surrounding the CR's winter pasture. Following it to the west, he came within a hundred yards of the ranch house just as Jim Radson was returning home after finishing his chores in the approaching darkness.

"I'll be damned—there he is!" exclaimed Jim as he remembered his last encounter with Charles. "That rotten critter laid me up for a week last fall. I ought to go get the rifle and shoot him!"

Charles, who was downwind of Jim, caught the scent of his former tormentor, whirled about, and trotted off into the woods behind the house.

Jim entered the house, and, as he was removing his outer clothing, related to his family how he'd just seen that "rotten red bull calf."

"The snow must have finally pushed him down off the mountain. I sure feel like shooting him after the way he laid me up."

"What a fine, charitable way to talk on Christmas Eve!" replied his wife.

"Well, at least I'm going to round him up and finish the job I started on him back then."

"We ought to be able to track him down in the snow and bring him in easy enough," said Jimmy, the eldest boy.

"Time enough for that later. Right now you'd better get in the bathroom and get cleaned up. We have to eat early in order to get into Eagle in time for church tonight," commanded Sue.

Luck and Charles's nocturnal tendencies managed to keep him apart from Jim throughout January and February. The only times

Jim saw Charles were on certain late evenings when the following night produced enough snow to hide his trail. On a few occasions Charles did come close enough to the house to be seen by Sue; close enough that she could see the botched brand on his flank that visibly read "Ch." Recognizing it as the abbreviation for "Charles," she started teasing her husband by referring to his slippery new adversary as Charles.

"Guess what, Jim? I saw Charles standing along the creek today."

"Damn!" was the reply.

"You know what? Charles was right up behind the house at the edge of the woods this morning."

"Damn, damn!"

Then, to make things even harder for Jim, Charles bumped into Harold and his herd of elk. Recognizing them as old friends, he started tagging along with them most of the time. Since he was only a little better than half grown, his hoof prints were about the same size as many of the full-grown elk, making him more difficult to track.

On the first night that he accompanied the elk to Jim's charitable handout of hay scattered along the fence line, Charles observed the elk leaping the fence with ease, and discovered that he could jump almost as well. Furthermore, remembering well what had happened to him the last time he was in that pasture, Charles was even more timid than Harold about emerging from the protective woods before dark.

One night in late March, Charles had accompanied the elk right up close to the barn to use the salt and mineral licks that Jim had out for his cattle. It was about ten P.M. and Jim had gone out with his electric lantern to check his brood cows for early calving. The calves weren't due until early April, but Jim, not wanting to lose a single one, was on guard early. As he came around the barn, Jim momentarily caught sight of Charles standing amidst the startled herd of elk. "Oh, hell, there he is again. How do you like that. Running around with the elk, wild as hell. I'm going to start carrying the rifle. It sure don't look like I'll ever be able to catch him any other way. Might as well butcher and eat the bugger as have him running around like an elk," exclaimed Jim as the elk and Charles dashed away.

Even his attempt to shoot Charles failed, since rancher Radson was a poor shot: one evening in early April he missed Charles by a good three feet at less than a hundred yards.

At the beginning of the second week of April, the snow on the mountainside, while less than the normal yearly accumulation, stood at an average depth of two feet. Three days of unusually warm weather turned that into six inches of soggy slush that was almost pure water. Heavy rain fell the following day, and, since the ground was frozen solid, both rain and melted snow ran down the mountainside in torrents. The creek in the valley overflowed its banks and carried much debris down into the reservoir, clogging the dam's overflow pipe. The rising water then ran over and partially cut through the earthen dam, causing a vast surge to race down the valley toward the CR Ranch. A great deal of CR fence was ripped up by the onrush of the debris-filled water. Even worse, eleven newborn calves were drowned in the resulting flood.

As the warm rain began to fall, something in the memory of the lead cow of the elk herd made her reason that the time was past due to ascend the mountain, and she started leading the herd up the mountainside, Charles and Harold in tow.

Jim Radson now had so many other problems to contend with that he completely forgot about his enemy, that wild yearling throwback aurochs named Charles.

CHAPTER 16

One of life's little ironies is that the virtuous are seldom rewarded for good deeds performed or temptations resisted during their lifetime here on earth. Bob Bine, upon returning home, was welcomed with open arms by his wife, while poor Smitty, as a reward for his fidelity, was treated badly by his.

Shortly after Smitty had left on the hunting trip, the furnace had quit. His wife, Barb, had to call her father over to re-light it. Later, the car had started balking, and she and the girls hadn't been able to get around as they wished. Since Smitty and Bob had quit hunting on Tuesday, why, Barb wondered, hadn't they come straight home? Her cousin had often driven from Denver back to Minnesota in a day and a half; therefore it shouldn't have taken them four days to get home. Smitty and Bob must have been off drinking and raising hell!

What could Smitty say? His wife seemed to have become an untamable shrew.

Back at work on the following Monday morning, in the plant and during breaks, neither Smitty nor Bob mentioned the side trip they'd taken on the way home. Bob certainly was not about to bring it up, for fear that Smitty might mention the one hundred fifty dollars that his bimbo had swiped, and Smitty was still smarting from the scolding he'd received from Barb. To make matters worse, when Koehler found out that they hadn't brought any elk home, he started claiming that they'd not even gone hunting. Rather, they'd spent all their time and money boozing and chasing squaws. Thus the trip was shortly forgotten by all—all but the ever-loving Barbara, who never ceased reminding poor Smitty how he'd let his family down.

Winter in Minnesota does not officially come until the twenty-first of December; however, as usual, bitter cold had set in by the second week of November. As the days shortened and Christmas neared, the workers in the packing plant were forced to work even longer hours. A bumper crop had depressed the price of corn for farmers, influencing the same farmers to overproduce hogs also. The resulting glut of hogs on the market promptly depressed the price of hogs—a truly vicious cycle for farmers, but not so for the packers.

Cheap hogs caused profits for the packers to soar, and management, in an effort to seize as much profit as possible, forced much overtime on its workers. Throughout December and January, Smitty and Bob never saw daylight, except for weekends. Both were entombed long before the sun rose and were not released until after it had set. And, as if that were not depressing enough to the workers, the union contract had run out. Negotiations with management seemed to be stalled, and there was talk of either a strike or a lockout.

The local union had recently merged with a national meat packers' union, which then had forced a new business agent onto the local. This agent was determined to win many new concessions from management, while management was determined to hold the line and, if necessary, break the union.

Christmas of 1975 found almost everyone in town worried. The president of the company was approaching retirement and the next chief executive officer could well be a young vice president named Paul Worthington, who seemed to be a fast-rising star.

Worthington's father had spent his rather short life in the plant trying to earn enough to keep his son in college. Unfortunately he didn't live long enough to see Paul graduate, as he died from a heart attack just two weeks before graduation. The company, seeing a good opportunity for local publicity, recruited and hired young Worthington shortly thereafter. Paul, unlike his likable father, soon turned out to be the most ruthless of sycophants. Within a very short time he managed to backstab his way into upper management. Each of his mentors in the company, impressed with what seemed to be his boundless energy and utter sincerity, was always surprised when Paul very soon managed to clamber over and above their bleeding bodies, leaving everyone else believing that this young fellow was foursquare, grassroots, and honest. Quite honestly, he was completely without scruples of any sort. Everyone, from the president of the company, J. D. Dalton, clear on down to the lowest of the employees, would soon suffer at the hands of Mr. Paul Worthington.

Of all the people he had trampled upon, there was just one who had come to understand and appreciate Paul for what he really was: that person was his wife. Having been used like everyone else, she was determined to be present when he finally reached the top in order to reap the financial benefits of a high-priced divorce settlement from a high-salaried CEO. Within two years she would prove herself to be more sanguinary than her bloodthirsty mate.

By mid-March the forced extra hours and the stultifying monotony of their wretched jobs were beginning to tell on everyone. A Sunday afternoon television promotional about pike fishing on the impounded lakes of South Dakota became the chief topic of conversation for all the workers in Smitty's work area who gathered together for breaks the following Monday and Tuesday. During the spring, walleyed pike, according to the South Dakota Bureau of Tourism, who'd sponsored the program, all swam upstream to spawn, and would be milling about in huge numbers just below the dam forming the next lake. The film showed fish being caught on every cast, which was more than Bob could stand. Right away he began hounding Smitty to go fishing in mid-April. Sheer boredom and his nagging wife finally made Smitty agree to go. They scheduled a three-day weekend trip to, of all places, the dam at Pierre, South Dakota.

The fishing trip, just like the previous hunting trip, didn't turn out exactly as Bob had planned. Upon arriving at Pierre about noon on Friday, and launching the boat onto the Missouri River, they discovered that the outboard motor wouldn't run. Neither of the butchers had enough mechanical ability to diagnose the problem, so they had to reload the boat on the trailer and drive back to Pierre in search of a mechanic, who soon determined that the problem was a gummed-up carburetor caused by Bob's failure to drain all the gasoline from the motor before placing it into winter storage.

The mechanic's shop happened to be within a block of the dime store, which caused Smitty to recall his conversation with LaVonne the previous fall. For lack of anything better to do while the motor was being repaired, Smitty decided to walk over and renew acquaintances. Upon entering the store and inquiring after LaVonne, he was told that she had found work at the state capitol building nearby and had left the store last January. While disappointed to have missed her, Smitty found he was also pleased to hear of her good fortune.

The fishing, when they finally got around to it late that afternoon, was not all that good. Several other boats were fishing below the dam, and few were catching anything. Evening found them with few fish and very tired. Both were satisfied merely to crawl into bed in Bob's camper and fall asleep early.

Saturday's fishing was little better, so they decided to have dinner at the D&E Cafe and then check out the happenings over at the Silver Spur. As luck would have it, Bob managed to zero in on a married woman whose husband happened to be a member of the band. The near disaster made Bob want to depart the Silver Spur long before closing time.

Shortly after noon on Sunday they departed for home with less than a limit of fish. That afternoon, as Bob slept and Smitty drove, Smitty thought a bit about his life to date. As he reviewed it, his marriage seemed based upon an early sexual attraction. Barb still had her figure, for which he was well pleased, but for some reason he no longer found her very attractive. Her ever-growing criticism had become a turnoff. By contrast, he'd often found himself fondly remembering his one conversation with LaVonne. That LaVonne was quite plain in appearance and rather chunky didn't seem to matter, which he found quite odd.

Even though Smitty had hoped for much better when he got home late Sunday evening, he found his wife already in bed fast asleep. As he slipped into bed he was less than grateful to be greeted with no more than a groan as she rolled over and away.

"What a crappy life!" thought Smitty as he in turn presented his back to her.

CHAPTER 17

The first of May found Charles and the elk herd again at the meadow high on the east side of the mountain. The previous mild winter had been kind to the elk—the herd now numbered twenty-four, counting all the newborn calves.

Charles was almost a year old and about three-fourths grown. He had just passed puberty, which in cattle occurs around the twelfth month of life. Unlike the previous spring, he now had no desire to romp about with the young elk, and simply watched the cavorting calves with indifference. Even though he possessed only one testicle, new cravings were beginning to bother him, and would continue to do so for the remainder of his life. Unlike Harold and his harem, who mated but once a year, female cattle menstruate every twenty-one days. Charles would be tormented year-round, as are the males of most species high on the evolutionary chain.

Male elk and cattle attempt to mate only when the female is willing. In the case of cattle, estrus lasts only a brief twelve to eighteen hours. The male simply waits until the female is receptive.

Given a bit of thought, one must truly wonder how some women can describe their male companion of the previous evening as "having behaved like an animal." Would that he might behave so honorably! In the animal world males do not waste their passions upon each other, nor do the females paint their faces or sculpt and shape their udders to entice the males. Evolution is no doubt still happening, but it seems to be doing so in a most bizarre way, and with scant rhyme or reason! Man is certainly guilty of interfering with the evolution of other species, and is probably also messing up — if not ending — his own.

With no help from man (recall his sire's peculiar parentage and his dam's heterogeneous mixture), Charles had reverted to type, both physically and mentally. Should he find the proper mate sometime during his lifetime, aurochs could resume that evolution promoted by nature's selection of the fittest, rather than the evolution dictated by man. For the remainder of his life Charles would exercise the intellect he possessed, to examine the situation and then take action with both intensity and purpose. Was there ever a successful man who performed differently? A good many unsuccessful ones did.

Since man first domesticated cattle, he selectively bred the descendants of the aurochs to the point where most of them could not survive without his help. The American bison still does quite well foraging for itself, but cattle of all types need more than nature provides to thrive. Without fodder and supplements put away for the winter by ranchers, Western ranch cattle would surely starve during the winter.

Charles's four stomachs were as efficient as those of his ancestors, and those of the bison, in the extraction of nourishment from roughage; as a result, he weighed 620 pounds on his first birthday. He would exceed 1,000 pounds by his second.

Furthermore, his horns had developed in the old way: erect and pointed menacingly forward. Presently they were eight inches in length. At the age of two they would be fourteen inches long, and finally eighteen inches at the age of three. Already they were sharp and lethal weapons. Unlike Harold's antlers, Charles's horns would not be shed annually. This spring Harold again looked and acted ridiculous, two velvet-encrusted bulbs supported on stalks protruding from the top of his head. His latest antlers were again so sore and tender that he behaved in the most cowardly manner. For about half the year aggressive acts were not for Harold, the noble bull elk.

Not so for Charles, who, for lack of anything better to do, did, at the beginning of the third week of May, follow the lead cow elk farther up the mountain above the timberline in her quest for the rich and nutritious new grass now sprouting there.

Jim Radson had also anticipated the new grass, and rode up the trail to mend the fence surrounding the mountaintop in preparation for bringing the cow and calf herd up for the summer. On his first day up, Jim rode around a clump of scrubby trees and happened onto the elk herd out in the open. Charles and Harold, as had become their wont, were lurking in the shadows of the trees. Not seeing Harold, Radson assumed he was looking at a different and larger elk herd.

With the previous winter's scant snowfall, the fence needed little repair. The grass grew lush and green, so Radson decided to bring his cows and calves up early. The bulls had been removed from the herd for some time to prevent calving in late winter. Radson would bring them up to be with the rest of the herd in mid-August for May calving.

Throughout the summer, Jim usually rode up to check the cattle every third day. His inspection trips were always in the afternoon, so he always missed seeing Charles, who, tired from his early-morning activities, usually spent late mornings and afternoons resting up after his amorous adventures. By mid-August he'd not only lost his virginity, but had also managed to impregnate seven heifers and four cows—not bad for a yearling bull with but one testicle!

Ironically and unknowingly, he'd managed to revenge himself for the harsh treatment he'd received from Jim Radson the previous fall: some of the rancher's cows would be dropping their calves into snowbanks as early as mid-March the following year.

CHAPTER 18

As required by the federal government's National Labor Relations Board, the union's new business agent filed a notice of intent to strike on May 1, which caused little concern among the packing plant's workers. After all, they reasoned, the local union and the company had a long-standing good relationship. Strikes, though threatened in the past, had always been averted. Ninety-three years before, the company had been founded by a shrewd man, who'd passed the leadership on to his son, who in turn had managed the affairs of the company even better than his father. Even now, that son's heirs owned 37 percent of the company. The board of directors had, however, deemed the third generation of heirs unfit to manage, and had selected J. D. Dalton, a fellow board member.

Dalton had spent his eighteen years as president of the company trying to emulate the father and son who'd directed operations of the plant since its beginning, with but little success. One of his biggest faults was that he despised touring the plant and visiting with the workers as his predecessors had always done. Dalton much preferred sitting in his luxurious office, heeding the advice of his staff, and checking the bottom lines of the balance sheets they prepared. A good, healthy dividend, in his opinion, would ensure his job a few more years; not that he needed the money, as he'd become a most wealthy man during his tenure as head of the company.

There had been times in the past few years when he'd toyed with the idea of retiring, but he was possessed of so little imagination that he could think of nothing else to do with his time. Throughout his years in charge, the plant had practically managed itself, so why should he not stay on and collect even more unearned wealth?

J. D. Dalton had neither the wit to hold the company together nor the wit to keep his wife at home. For the past ten years, in the absence of an attentive husband, she had discovered the joy of touring Europe in quest of youth and youthful lovers. It seemed Dalton's wife had as little interest in him as Barb now had in Smitty, though it could be said in Barb's favor that she didn't lavish her attentions on anyone other than herself and her two daughters. Smitty's life was now being made miserable by two things: his wife's sharp tongue and the sheer boredom of his stupid job. When, in mid-May, Bob Bine suggested another elk-hunting trip, Smitty quickly coughed up the hundred-dollar fee now required for a Colorado non-resident hunting license, which arrived in his mailbox on the same day that the union's business agent, having convinced the membership of its necessity, called for a strike to begin the next Monday.

Unfortunately for all the workers, their new business agent had ulterior motives. His plan was to win a few benefits plus a small wage increase for the workers, and, with that feather in his hat, soon move up to and further into the national union's hierarchy.

Even more unfortunately for all concerned, Paul Worthington, the newly appointed director to the company's board, would behave similarly. Worthington's ploy was to develop a strategy that would break the union, thus enabling him to jump ahead of all the other board members in their efforts to replace J. D. Dalton as chief executive.

That the union would actually strike caught everyone in town by surprise and pleased hardly anyone. The workers, with all the overtime money in their pockets, were not hurting financially, and, having never before had to strike against the company, were uneasy about doing so.

The stockholders and heirs who owned the company disliked the publicity of a strike, and even more feared the strike might cut into the handsome dividends they were earning.

Dalton, the president, having throughout his life always refused to make a decision on his own, was the most uneasy and most susceptible to the advice of his newest and most ambitious young protégé. Dalton felt that Worthington's having been raised by a father who had labored in the plant made him the most qualified person on his staff to deal with the union employees, whom he himself understood not at all. Worthington was, in actuality, quite the opposite of what Dalton perceived him to be. Worthington had developed with such rapacity that he would do anything—short of getting caught doing it—to achieve his goal.

Initially the strike went well for the workers. Picket lines were established at all entrance gates to the plant with no violence. Having never manned picket lines before, most of the workers felt rather embarrassed at having to do so. Unfortunately, negotiations, when resumed, quickly broke down. Worthington, who'd been given the job of chief negotiator for the company, shortly assumed as rigid a position as did his union counterpart.

At the next board meeting, J. B. Dalton declared a large dividend for the stockholders, and large pay raises and increased stock options for both himself and his corporate staff. Then, fearing repercussions from his actions, he decided to accompany his wife on one of her European vacations, thus making nobody happy, especially his wife. Well, almost nobody—Worthington was most happy for having been left in charge, and promptly leaked the executive pay raises to the press, which infuriated the striking workers.

Those manning the picket lines soon became abusive, shouting threats at both management and the maintenance workers who daily had to cross the lines. Local grocers noticed an increase in the sale of eggs, of which a good many were thrown at Worthington's car when he crossed the picket line on the following morning. Capitalizing on the incident, Worthington made a phone call to the press to be sure they would be present to film the same throwing as he left the plant that afternoon.

His next move was to phone the governor of the state, whom he'd been cultivating, and ask if he'd care to ride along on the company jet to Monterey, California, for a weekend of golf at Pebble Beach, since he (Worthington) was going out there on business anyway. Seizing upon the opportunity to play such a prestigious course, the governor, a rabid golfer and an avid drinker, accepted the invitation, and thereby would subject himself to a great deal of propaganda while in a most pliable (semi-inebriated) state of mind.

The important business that the company jet delivered Worthington to California for was really just an excuse to spend time with the governor to gain his support against the union. The governor and his aide were delivered to the course for an afternoon round of golf, while Worthington was off to visit a small condiment supplier that supplied spices to the packing plant for seasoning sausages and such. The condiment company's manager was absolutely amazed at having a visit from a big chief who had little, if any, knowledge about the use of seasoning.

"Cripes! Why didn't he just send for our catalogue?" was the man's comment as Worthington departed after only slightly more than an hour.

Not wishing to let the governor know how little time he'd spent on business, Worthington spent the remainder of the afternoon at a beach-side bar in Carmel, before his scheduled dinner with the governor. Young women cavorting about the beach in skimpy bathing suits made Worthington aware of how unbalanced his hormonal level had become; when a prostitute plying her profession caught his attention, he arranged a liaison following his dinner engagement, leaving her with a deposit for her services and the key to his hotel room.

During their evening meal, Worthington saw to it that the governor was filled with both alcohol and his version of the labor problems back at the packing plant. Furthermore, he lent a sympathetic ear to the governor's problems with an obstinate legislature. He also let it be known that his business had gone so well that he was available for golf the following day.

On the Saturday morning following, Worthington found himself surprised that, despite his strenuous sexual activities and sleepless night, he had to concentrate on losing the golf match with the governor, who was a hack! During their lunch break and before their scheduled afternoon round of golf, a waiter whom he'd bribed to do so summoned Worthington to the phone for a nonexistent call. Upon returning to the table, he informed the governor that they'd best forgo the afternoon game because of information he'd just received concerning possible violence back at the plant.

During the three-hour jet ride back to Minnesota, while having the steward keep the governor well supplied with booze (the governor was a lush!), Worthington managed to impress upon the governor how similar their jobs were: great responsibility and little recognition for their efforts. By the time they reached St. Paul, the governor's aide had to help him off the plane because of his condition.

On the short hop from the state capital back home, Worthington reviewed his efforts of the previous days and considered them all successful but for the tryst with his whore. He became convinced that she had just pretended satisfaction.

While Worthington returned from his trip to California on Saturday evening relatively pleased, events that had confronted Smitty the previous few days left him far less than pleased. Friday evening, Barb had informed him that she no longer loved him, never had loved him, was going to sue him for divorce, that he should move himself and all his belongings out of the house as soon as possible, and that he must sleep on the living room sofa until he complied with all her wishes.

What could he, a sensitive introvert, say?

CHAPTER 19

By July, all the workers had lost five weeks' wages, far more money than they would have gained in five years if given the wage increase they were demanding (a fact they all chose to ignore). Someone among them had calculated that the pay raises taken by management exceeded the wage demands of the union, which was almost but not quite true. Pickets were becoming angry and mouthy. Mornings and evenings, Worthington looked out his office window and smiled as he watched J. D. Dalton, now returned from Europe without his wife, cross the picket line while being showered with eggs and angry shouts.

With the offering of a very large campaign contribution from the company's coffers, plus the explanation that his company was already exceeding the industry's standard for wages, Worthington was able to acquire the aid of the governor. He didn't mention to the governor that much of the industry he was speaking of was the beef-packing industry located in the Southwestern states, where they were already employing low-paid Mexican migrant workers, who were often in the United States illegally. Worthington's plant mainly butchered hogs; however they still slaughtered some beef (bologna bulls), which they ground along with pork to manufacture specialty meats such as bologna. So far as the plant was concerned, the beef kill was a small operation, employing only twenty-eight workers. Worthington was of the opinion that they could buy all the beef needed from plants operating in the Southwest far cheaper than it cost them to butcher their own. Furthermore, he believed that he'd someday be able to employ cheap migrant labor himself, but that would be several years in the future.

In the meantime, having been prompted by Worthington, the governor, after a series of properly timed press releases, called out the National Guard "To restore law and order to the community," even though there'd been no serious violence to date.

Smitty, throughout all this labor strife, also had to cope with his impending divorce, and had trouble handling the situation. A local judge had ordered him to pay child support and maintain the family's expenses, until he, the judge, would issue a final divorce decree. Smitty's lawyer had little interest in the case other than demanding that his own fee be paid regularly. With no source of income other than the strike fund, Smitty found himself in dire financial trouble, for which the judge had threatened to throw him into jail!

The presence of the National Guard outside the plant broke the strike. The sympathy of the general public had fallen behind management. Local merchants, faced with declining sales, became worried about the condition of their own purses. Even the churches, when faced with declining contributions, began urging the workers back to work, and of course most of the company shareholders, facing the prospect of lost earnings on their stock, urged all the workers to return.

J. B. Dalton, as usual, listened to and abided by the wishes of his staff. Worthington's manipulations had been so effective that he was treated as a hero by his peers on the board of directors; as a result, the decision of the board was to go ahead and stick it to the union. Therefore they made a public offer to hire back anyone who would cross the picket line (at a slightly reduced wage, of course).

That offer did completely tear the community asunder. Naturally, many of the workers became furious at the offer to go back to work for less than they'd been making before the strike. The local farmers, taking a financial beating because of their own over-production of pork, were quick to single out the union as being responsible for their problems. The southern Minnesota town in which the packing plant was located was a single-industry town of only 20,000, surrounded by several other more rural villages that were little more than bedroom communities for packing-plant workers. Filial as well as union brothers became enemies, who either refused to attend family picnics or, if they did attend, refused to speak to each other.

Even the union became divided. The national union was reluctant to continue supporting the local union for wage demands that were already higher than anything being paid to any other local. The national began withholding strike funds from the local.

Violence did begin to happen, but was directed away from management, who were well protected by the police, and onto union members who'd given up on the strike and gone back to work. Those who'd even spoken in favor of ending the strike became objects of scorn. Even more scorned was a new group who'd just appeared on the scene.

Toward the end of the strike, management had advertised for new employees and had begun hiring to replace those who chose to remain on strike. These new employees became the recipients of most of the violence and mischief. Tires were slashed, windows were broken, and front lawns were ruined by pouring liquid herbicide onto them to spell the word, "SCAB."

Some of those who returned to work had been forced to do so by circumstances, such as Bob Bine, whose daughter suffered from a congenital defect and who was uninsurable by any coverage other than that provided by the company. Also, some of those who'd returned to work did so after having been told by their bankers either to go back to work or suffer the consequences of mortgage foreclosure and eviction. Smitty was forced back into the plant by the district court judge who said, "Start paying child support and alimony or go to jail."

The strike dwindled to a close, leaving the local union defeated, management victorious, and all but Mr. Paul Worthington with a bad taste in their mouths.

Once the plant began operating again, J. B. Dalton chose to retire as president and to remain onboard as the highly paid chairman of the board. To the surprise of hardly any, he chose Paul Worthington to be the new company president. All of Worthington's peers on the board, not understanding his true character, would soon regret ratifying his appointment.

Worthington, having achieved his goal of several years, and while shopping in the town's ritziest department store with his wife, chanced onto one of his failed conquests, upon whom he would now focus all of his selfish designs. She happened to be a high school girlfriend of years gone by, who just happened to be in the store at the same time looking at fancy goods that she could not afford. The conquest of that elusive and animate object would cost Worthington dearly in far more ways than he could afford.

The object of his latest passion just happened to be Smitty's estranged wife Barbara!

CHAPTER 20

On the first of August, Jim Radson and his two sons moved Black Hercules and the other four bulls up to the mountaintop summer pasture. According to Jim's calculations, cows bred on the first of August would calve on May sixth the following year, which in his estimation would be the proper time, as May weather would be warm enough for new calves to survive.

All five of the bulls had spent the spring and summer together so they probably would not fight once put in with the cows. Furthermore, they were either polled or had been dehorned, so any fight over cows in heat would amount to little more than a shoving match.

Once the bulls had been introduced to the herd, Radson decided to patrol the fence surrounding the bald mountaintop. Halfway around they came upon Harold, the noble elk, and his harem. The sight of all the elk caused the boys to become excited about the forthcoming hunting season.

"How about it, Dad? Do we get to go along this year? asked Jimmy, the youngest.

"Depends on how well you do in school," Jim's replied. Then he commented that Harold wasn't fleshed out very well and appeared to be a bit beyond his prime. "Boys, I think old Harold is about done for. I'll bet he's at least fourteen years old. He looks pretty gaunt. Probably be just as well if Bob and Smitty get him this fall."

As they were closing the gate prior to heading back down the trail to the ranch house, they failed to notice Charles, who had been watching them from the shadows of some tree-line spruce. As usual, Charles had been spending the day resting and ruminating, having reverted to the aurochs habit of grazing at night and resting most of the day.

That evening, coming out of the woods to rejoin the herd, he was confronted by his sire, Black Hercules, who worked himself up into a rage because of the intrusion of this small and skinny young bull, whom he recognized as a rival suitor rather than as his offspring. (That wouldn't have made any difference to Hercules anyway.) Once thoroughly enraged, Hercules lowered his massive head and charged. After nimbly dodging several attacks by this ponderous mountain of black flab, Charles recognized Hercules's weaknesses—stupidity and clumsiness—and decided to take him on. Following each headlong attack, Charles would dance nimbly aside, and then gouge Hercules in the flank with his horns. Ten such charges left Black Hercules gasping for breath and bleeding profusely from his left flank. The scent of blood now really excited Charles, and he, in turn, assumed the offensive.

It didn't take Charles long to defeat his huge, flabby opponent. In less than five minutes Hercules was on his knees, and five more saw him lying helplessly on his side, dying, lungs punctured and entrails spewing out of a gored paunch. Finally, Charles realized that all the fight was gone from Hercules; he gave up mauling his dying father to trot proudly off to the herd and claim all his prizes.

Early the following day, when Jim Radson returned to the pasture to check on the herd, he came across his prize bull lying quite dead in a pool of congealed blood. Off in the distance he happened to see Charles mounting one of his cows, and figured out what had happened. Completely losing his head, Jim yanked his thirty-thirty carbine out of its scabbard and galloped his horse straight at Charles, intending to shoot him. Fortunately for Charles, Jim was so enraged that he started screaming curses as he galloped. His noisy charge alerted Charles to danger, and he quickly gave up his pleasure and hightailed it for the nearest woods. Jim fired a wild shot that didn't even come close, and was then neatly thrown from his horse, who'd been frightened by having a gun fired over his head. Limping and cursing, Jim retrieved his rifle and his horse. Finally realizing how he'd let his temper get the best of him, he vowed to return every day until he managed to kill that "sons-a-bitchin', rotten, red, one-nutted, scrawny, no good, shittin' bull!"

Throughout the remainder of August, Jim never managed to catch Charles within range of his carbine. He did fire at him three times but missed each time. Concluding that he needed a rifle with greater range, Jim bought a scope-sighted, high-powered rifle, and even practiced shooting it. All his efforts had merely made Charles more elusive. Once Jim acquired the new rifle, he never laid eyes on Charles again. His daily presence did, however, manage to keep Charles away from the herd and the other bulls. Charles ceased coming out of the woods by daylight throughout the month of September. In the final week of the month, a light snow fell at higher elevations, and, with forecasts of early major snowfall, Radson moved his cattle down to winter pasture earlier than usual—most of them, that is, since Charles was holding three cows hostage halfway down the mountainside at his meadow.

This year the elk season was held early again: the second Saturday in October was opening day. Bob and Smitty had planned to leave home Wednesday night after work in order to arrive at the CR Ranch one day ahead of the opening. The next Monday, however, Bob's daughter became very ill and was admitted to the hospital for surgery. Bob, of course, had to stay home. On Tuesday, after the operation, he called the Radsons to explain the situation.

Sue took the call; after she'd repeated to her husband what had happened to her cousin, Jim asked for the phone. He told Bob that he sure was sorry to hear of the surgery, that they were pleased that all appeared well with Bob's daughter, that he understood why Bob couldn't come, and that for sure he should come the next year. He also said that Smitty should come anyhow, and that he'd be able to hunt with him, as the calves had not been sold yet due to poor prices. Jim even asked for Smitty's phone number and called him to extend a personal invitation, which Smitty accepted.

Wednesday morning, Smitty called his corner gas station to have his old pickup tuned and a new set of tires installed. Wednesday evening after work, just as he and Bob had planned, he threw all his gear in the back and headed for Colorado. By driving almost constantly and sleeping briefly at rest stops along the freeway, he managed to arrive at the CR Ranch late Friday afternoon, the day before elk season, where he was welcomed by Jim and Sue Radson.

Jim, having made almost daily trips to the mountaintop for the past month and a half, felt that he could locate the elk herd with but little effort, and that a scouting trip up the mountain was unnecessary. They did drive up to the campsite by the reservoir to see if the same hunters were there again this year, and they were. Just like the previous year they were busy becoming obnoxiously drunk.

"I'd like to be able to go over there and tell them to keep the hell off my land, but all the land up the mountain is leased from the federal government, and dammit, I can't legally keep 'em off it."

"From the looks of them now, they probably won't be up and around very early tomorrow anyhow," observed Smitty.

"We won't take any chances. We'll leave before daylight and not give them a chance to spoil our hunt," said Jim.

Upon returning to the ranch, Jim broke the bad news to his sons that they had to stay home to do the chores on Saturday morning, so that Smitty and he could leave early enough to beat the other hunters up the mountain. He did promise that they could come along Sunday morning, and that the eldest could carry the thirty-thirty.

Early October daylight does not arrive until shortly before seven A.M. At five A.M., Smitty was shivering both with anticipation and the cold as he prepared to climb aboard his horse for the trip up the mountain.

"Good thing the moon is still up so we'll be able to see the trail," said Jim as he showed Smitty how to attach the saddlebag containing lunch to the rear of his saddle. "You'll have to carry your rifle slung across your back again as I don't have a scabbard it would fit in. Just be sure not to fire the blamed thing off that gelding's back, or I guarantee you that he'll throw you halfway back down the mountain. He did it to me. Actually, he's a good riding horse, and he'll give you a much better ride than old Bell did last year."

Halfway up they paused to rest the horses, and Jim said, "I suppose I ought to be rolling a cigarette now before passing profound words of wisdom on to you, but I don't smoke — never could stand the damned things. I expect we'll find the elk herd lying on a point facing east, soaking up the warm morning sun. At least that's where I usually find 'em. Hopefully, we'll be able to spot them before they see us, and be able to sneak up on them. The wind is in the right direction today. Do you want a big old trophy bull, or good eating meat?"

Smitty laughed, "Since I don't have a family to feed anymore, guess I'll go for the big antlers."

"Fine with me," commented Jim. "Old Harold's about at the end of his rope anyhow, and he sure has a large rack. As for me, I want a nice young cow for the meat."

For once in his life everything went as Jim planned. Sure enough, the elk were where he'd predicted they'd be. He and Smitty tied their horses at the timberline and made a successful stalk, finally crawling to within 175 yards of the herd.

"Take the bull," whispered Jim. "I'll get my cow right after you shoot."

Harold hardly knew what hit him. Smitty's first shot plowed through both his chest and his heart. He simply rolled over onto his side. Jim fired immediately afterward and the herd bounded away, leaving both Harold and a young cow lying on the ground, kicking spasmodically.

"I can't believe it! Seven-thirty and the season's all over for us!" said Smitty in amazement.

"It's just beginning," said Jim. "Now we have to butcher these critters and pack 'em back down the mountain!"

By the time the two elk were disemboweled and dragged down the mountain to a tree large enough for them to be hung and skinned, it was noon.

"A horse can pack out two quarters," said Jim, "so we'll come back tomorrow with all four horses and pack the meat out. No, that won't work either. I forgot about the head and antlers."

"Why don't you take back two quarters on my horse today? Smitty offered. Then we could haul all the rest back tomorrow. Besides, I'd like to hike back down through that slide meadow where we found that old cow and calf last year, just to see it again."

"That calf, as you may recall, has caused me more than a bunch of pain and trouble. He grew up and the damned bastard killed that expensive Angus bull of mine. If you should come across him, I'd be obliged if you'd shoot him on the spot."

It took them another hour to cut the cow in half and load the two hindquarters onto Smitty's mount for the trip back to the ranch. When Smitty finally saw Jim loaded and off toward the trail, he hiked over to the proper ridge and began his descent to the meadow. He reached it about two P.M., and, pausing in the shadows before entering, he saw Charles and three CR cows by the spring at its upper end.

One of those cows looks almost exactly like that old mother of Charles that I had to shoot last fall, mused Smitty.

There was an excellent reason for the resemblance: she was Charles's half sister, whom he'd recently impregnated.

Disregarding Jim's request to shoot Charles on sight, Smitty skirted down and around the meadow to the trail across the slide, keeping out of Charles's sight all the while. When Smitty finally arrived back at the ranch that evening, he told the Radsons that he'd seen Charles and three cows at the slide meadow, but hadn't shot Charles because he was with the others, which he didn't want to scatter. He suggested to Jim that the boys accompany them up the next day with all four horses, all of which could be used to pack the other six quarters of elk plus Harold's trophy head back down. He (Smitty) and the boys would again drive the cattle down to the winter pasture as they had the year before. Jim could again open the fence to drive Charles and the three cows through.

"Oh, okay, I guess. I still wish you'd have shot that damned Charles!" exclaimed Jim.

"Oh, come on, Jim!" said Sue. "Be reasonable. If you could get him down here you could sell him at the auction in Eagle on Monday morning. At least we'd be getting something for him. After all, John Colvin owns half of him, you know."

Overnight it snowed slightly down at the ranch, but, upon ascending to the mountaintop, they found the snow to be eight inches deep. All helped Jim load the remaining six elk quarters onto three of the horses. Harold's head, complete with its huge rack of antlers, was lashed onto Jim's horse. The horses were then tied together in a string, and Jim set out on foot leading his pack train back down to the ranch.

Smitty and the boys waited two hours before heading over to the appropriate finger ridges to drive Charles and his harem back down the mountainside. As things worked out, Smitty had no trouble driving Charles and his retinue out of the meadow and across the shale slide, although Smitty almost deposited his bones alongside those of Old Maude while crossing the slippery snow-covered trail across the slide.

With much shouting, the boys managed to prevent the cattle from returning to the mountaintop. All then proceeded down the ridge, through the opened winter pasture fence, and on into the corral near the barn. So long as he was with his harem, Charles remained rather docile. Once Jim had Charles in the corral, he took no chances and loaded him directly into the livestock trailer to be sold the following Monday.

Monday, Smitty hung around the ranch, helped Jim with the chores, and accompanied him to the sales barn where Charles was sold to an order buyer for a pittance. Charles would be shipped to a feedlot in a small Minnesota town near Smitty's packing plant to be fattened for slaughter as a bologna bull.

Later that day, even though he couldn't afford it, Smitty took all the Radsons out to dinner at Eagle's finest, and only, restaurant.

By Tuesday morning the temperature had fallen into the low twenties, and Smitty decided to head for home and the drudgery that awaited him there. They loaded Harold's frozen carcass, which Smitty intended to share with Bob Bine, into the back of Smitty's pickup, along with the head and antlers.

"As cold as it is, everything should stay frozen so long as you keep it covered with this tarp during the day," Jim observed.

Bidding everyone a fond farewell, Smitty departed for home. Well, not quite. That evening he decided to return by way of Pierre, South Dakota, after having called ahead from Denver to arrange a date with LaVonne DeLorme.

CHAPTER 21

Smitty had somewhat reluctantly left the Radsons' Tuesday afternoon and arrived in Denver late that evening. It was from the cheap motel where he stayed overnight that he phoned LaVonne and begged for a date for Wednesday evening.

The surprise of a long-distance call from Colorado from someone she'd met only briefly a year before piqued LaVonne's curiosity enough to accept Smitty's invitation to dinner. As arranged over the phone, Smitty was to meet her under the rotunda of the capitol building in Pierre at four-thirty on Wednesday when she got off work.

This sure ought to be different, LaVonne thought after hanging the phone up. *At least I won't be going out with a married man. Well, almost not married, as he said he was separated and the divorce was almost final. From what I can remember, he was a polite and rather sensitive fellow. Different from all the other guys I've met in the Silver Spur. They couldn't wait for the place to close up before trying to rush me off and into bed. I wonder why his wife wanted to get rid of him? Maybe he's just another nut. Oh, well. I haven't had a date for nearly a year. Why not?* she thought as she climbed into bed for the evening.

Back at the Denver motel, Smitty also pulled the covers up around his neck and nodded off in pleasant anticipation of his forthcoming date with LaVonne. Unfortunately, several times during the night, his pleasant dreams were interrupted by bad ones in which his former mate was berating him. Three times he pleasantly drifted off to sleep imagining LaVonne at his side, and three times he awoke in a sweat hearing Barbara screeching at him. The third time, at a quarter of five in the morning, Smitty awoke himself by shouting, "For God's sake, Barbara, leave me alone. It's Saturday, I don't have to go to work today!" Finally realizing where he was, he thought, *Oh for crap's sake, she kicked me out five months ago. Why in hell do I have to continually be plagued with all this shit?*

Part of the reason Smitty awoke so early was because of his job. Five days a week he had to be on the line and working by six A.M. His internal alarm clock had been adjusted by others to go off at five every morning.

Guess I'd just as well get up and get going. It's about four hundred and fifty miles to Pierre and I'm supposed to be there by four-thirty this afternoon, he thought as he staggered out of bed and into the shower, where, having been the first in that flea-bag motel to awake, there was adequate hot water. (A bit later it would become a scarce commodity.)

After a long and noisy shower, in the course of which he managed to wake up the trucker in the next room, Smitty dressed and went out to warm his truck before packing and leaving at five. He never woke up hungry, so he decided to drive a bit before breakfast, and managed to get some one hundred miles along Interstate 80 before the sun crept above the horizon. Although he still wasn't hungry, he pulled in for breakfast at Ft. Morgan, Colorado—which lies alongside the south branch of the Platte River—rather than drive on into the early-morning sun. During breakfast, Smitty decided to retrace his route back along the Platte River, through Nebraska, to North Platte, and then head straight north to South Dakota. He'd traveled that particular stretch along the Platte twice before, but at night both times.

Visually, the Platte was not at all what he'd expected; it appeared to be just a small stream meandering through a wide valley. Had he traveled this route some 125 years ago, along with the wagon trains of that era, he'd have seen twice the water, since half of the flow was now being used for irrigation.

Upon reaching the town of North Platte, he left the interstate and drove north through Nebraska's desolate sand-hill country, reaching the South Dakota border shortly before noon. Arriving in Pierre at what he thought was three P.M., he discovered he'd crossed a time zone. It was already four. Changing shirts and donning a sweater at a truck stop, Smitty reached the capitol rotunda with but five minutes to spare. While loitering about he noticed a lead plaque on display in a case that read, PIERRE LA VÉRENDRYE, 1742.

A couple of boys playing on the east bank of the Missouri River had discovered the plaque in Pierre back in 1913.

1742? I wonder if Pierre was named for him? How could that be? Lewis and Clark didn't mention the place when they came by here much later, Smitty mused. He was so engrossed with the plaque that he almost didn't recognize LaVonne when she arrived, for she'd lost considerable weight and now wore her dark hair quite short.

"Hello, Smitty," smiled LaVonne. "You look exactly like I remembered you."

Well, you don't," replied Smitty. "Your hair is short and you've lost some weight. LaVonne, you really look great!"

"Oh, I've been working on it. I managed to get rid of some flab. How do you like the smile now?" she laughed, pointing to the replaced missing tooth. "Money can buy anything."

"LaVonne, believe me, you really look great!"

"You be careful, Smitty. I'll have you know that I'm susceptible to flattery. Well, now, what are your plans for this evening?"

"Goll, I don't know. I forgot about the time change and didn't get here in time to even find a motel yet. I'd like to go out for a rather fancy meal at a nice quiet restaurant but I haven't the vaguest idea where to go. This is your town, so just name it and be my guest. Unfortunately, I didn't bring a suit and tie." At this point, Smitty was somewhat shocked at his ability to converse so well or so long.

"For clothes, most anything goes around here. Just take a look at some of these guys in this hall. Would you believe that they're senators and lawyers in jeans and cowboy boots? You look just fine in what you're wearing. I'd like to change, though. I live within walking distance. Would you mind driving me there?"

"I'd love to."

Just as they were going out the door of the capitol, a tall, thin fellow in Western garb caught up with them and said, "Hi, LaVonne. Who's your friend?"

"Bill, this is Loren Smith. "Smitty, this beanpole is Bill Verstegn, my boss. You'd never know it by looking at him, but he's our state attorney general."

"Hi, Smitty," Bill said, grabbing him by the hand as they all walked toward the parking lot. "Where you from?"

"Southeastern Minnesota."

"Really? What brings you out to this God-awful country?"

"I wouldn't call it that. It's big and empty, all right, but I sort of like it here. I'm on my way home from a Colorado elk-hunting trip."

"Any luck?"

"Yeah, I got a big old bull with a huge set of antlers."

"Let's have a look," Bill said as they approached Smitty's truck.

Smitty opened the door of the topper on the back of his truck and uncovered Harold's head with its massive antlers.

"Boy, you ain't kidding. Would I ever like to have that hanging in my office!"

"Well, you can't have it," joked LaVonne. "One dead head in your office is enough."

"Impudent woman!" sniffed Bill. "Smitty, I'll leave you now.

My own good woman is waiting for me at home with my slippers and a hot toddy by the fireplace. Nice to have met you, Smitty. You be careful now, or LaVonne'll have your hair hanging on a pole in front of her teepee."

LaVonne's teepee, as Smitty observed upon arriving there, was a tastefully furnished three-room apartment in a condominium only three blocks from the capitol building.

"Sorry I haven't anything to drink. There might be some pop in the refrigerator if you want it. I'll go change now."

"That's okay. I can wait," replied Smitty while observing the neatness of her apartment and mentally comparing it to the usual disarray of his own.

Dinner at Michael's went extremely well. Smitty unknowingly let LaVonne draw him out on his separation and forthcoming divorce. Quite surprisingly, Smitty found himself able to talk about it freely, something he'd never been able to do with anyone before.

In turn, LaVonne found herself surprised that Smitty was neither angry nor bitter about the breakup. She was both angry and disgusted with her own drunken ex. Without realizing it they spent nearly three hours at the restaurant and didn't leave until nine.

LaVonne had driven her car rather than take Smitty's "hearse," as she called his pickup truck loaded with Harold's carcass. Once back at the apartment, Smitty was invited in for even more coffee.

"I'd better go look for a motel before it gets too late," Smitty said.

"You could sleep on the sofa and save the cost of a motel."

Smitty spent the night at LaVonne's—he didn't sleep on the sofa.

The following morning Smitty awoke to find LaVonne already awake and lying close by his side. Looking at his watch he said,

"Good God, LaVonne! It's nine-thirty. You're going to be late for work on account of me!"

"That's okay. I'm going to quit working and you're going to take me back to live with you in your mansion," she teased.

"What!"

"Guess what? Today is Columbus Day. All us bureaucrats take the day off to honor good-old Christopher for stealing the continent from the locals. I don't work today. Isn't that nice?"

"Oh, Lord, yes," sighed Smitty. "Now I can just stay here in bed with you. I don't think I'll go back home to my crappy job. I'll stay and help you spend your inheritance."

"Ha! We could spend that in less than a month. It's curious you should say that, though, as I was going to go out and visit my ma this afternoon. Want to go along? You'd get a chance to see my inheritance. All eighty acres of it."

"Hm, maybe later. Right now I want to look at something else."

"You listen here, buster! These covers stay up around my neck. I'm fat and ugly."

"Lemme check and see."

"You do and your damned scalp will shortly be hanging over that bedpost!"

"Oh, okay! Right now I don't want to decide whether or not to go along to your ma's. I want to do something else."

That afternoon Smitty did drive LaVonne's car out to her mother's farm. Her brother, Tom, his wife, and their five kids were there also. For a while, until Tom took pity on him and drew him from the kitchen out into the living room, Smitty felt quite awkward. Shortly after they arrived, LaVonne and her mother fell into a rather heated argument in the Lakota Sioux tongue. About the only word that Smitty recognized was *washiska,* which he believed meant "paleface."

A translation of the conversation would read:

Mom: "Why in hell are you running around with a damned paleface anyhow?"

LaVonne: "It's none of your business. I like him."

Mom: "There's all kinds of nice fellows over on the reservation."

LaVonne: "Oh sure! A bunch of G.D. drunks. Aren't you forgetting about the one I married? He knocked my teeth out."

Mom: "Well, that's because he wasn't Sioux. He was part Arikara."

LaVonne: "Oh, go to hell! Aren't you forgetting that Dad was part French?"

Mom: "That's different. He was Metis."

LaVonne: "Ma, I'm going to live my own life the way I want to live it!"

Mom: "It's just not right."

LaVonne (in English): "Oh, just shut up!"

To Smitty's relief, Tom had none of his mother's prejudices. If he had any at all, he kept them well concealed. Tom worked as a maintenance man for Hyde County, operating a road grader in the summer and a snowplow in the winter. The wages he earned for his efforts were decent enough for South Dakota, but with a wife and five kids there was little left over from each weekly paycheck. Tom had never lived on the reservation; for that matter, he'd never been more than one hundred miles from his hometown of Highmore, South Dakota. A big trip for Tom and his family, which happened no more than twice a year, was only to Pierre. Tom found it quite fascinating that Smitty had been clear out to Colorado on a successful elk-hunting trip.

While driving back to Pierre after having finally left LaVonne's mother's place, Smitty asked LaVonne if Tom might accept half of the elk, for all along he had planned to give half of it to his buddy Bob Bine. Now that he had lost both his house and deep freezer, he didn't even have a place to store the meat.

LaVonne said, "Probably, but Sioux custom dictates that Tom would then have to give you something in return."

"Oh, hell! I've already got his sister, haven't I? That's more than enough. Tom saw that and didn't object. Your Ma sure did, though, didn't she?"

"Smitty, I've noticed something about you: you're awfully perceptive. You figured Ma out right away, didn't you? Well, there's nothing I can do about her. She's always tried to run our lives for us. Are you surprised to find out that minorities have prejudices too?"

"Not really."

Focusing directly on Smitty, LaVonne said, "You saw your divorce coming on, didn't you?"

"Yeah, I guess I did."

"Did you do anything to prevent it?"

"Oh, Christ, yes! But she never listened. Seems like that's always been the case with me. Try as I might, I can't seem to get anyone to listen to what I'm trying to say. No, I shouldn't say that. I think you're the only person I've ever met that seems to care enough to really listen. I noticed that about you the first time we met a year ago. I couldn't talk to Barb at all. She never listened. You do."

Moving closer, LaVonne said, "My ex and I didn't talk either. If things didn't go his way he'd just kick hell out of me."

"We've got something in common there. You got kicked around, I got kicked out."

"At least you didn't lose any teeth, Smitty."

"True, but you walked out. I got thrown out."

"Smitty, it wasn't easy leaving. For the longest time I felt like it was my fault, that I ought to be able to make it all work. Finally, it dawned on me that it wasn't my fault, and I left. He didn't give a damn. Big surprise! I was even more surprised to find that I didn't give a damn either. I was luckier than you, Smitty. I didn't have any kids."

By the time they reached Pierre, it had become quite dark and had begun to snow lightly. Once inside the apartment, LaVonne switched the TV on for the evening news, which announced that the first blizzard of the year was about to begin.

CHAPTER 22

Smitty and LaVonne reluctantly parted company at nine AM on the following Sunday. The blizzard really only prevented his leaving for one day. He could have left on Saturday but didn't. Smitty went home by way of Highmore to make good his promise to deliver half of old Harold's carcass to LaVonne's brother and his family, while LaVonne, a devout Catholic, went to confession where she tearfully confessed her recent sins. Had the old priest, who heard her out, known and understood how lonely she had been for most of her life he, whiled granting absolution, surely would have advised her that her sins were minor. Old and worldly wise only through his own love for food and wine he finished with, "Sin no more, my daughter," then waddled off to his lunch.

The weather as Smitty was driving home was bitter cold—fifteen degrees below zero. The sky was heavily overcast, and the scanty output of the truck's heater added greatly to poor Smitty's misery. Supposed to have been back at work on Friday, he had overstayed his vacation, and now wondered what his new foreman would have to say when he showed up Monday.

On Monday morning he got by with no more than a bawling out in front of his fellow workers, all of whom were most sympathetic. Asked why he was so late getting back, he lied by claiming to have been caught in a blizzard for three days. During the first break of the day, Koehler, his nasty coworker—with no perception other than the workings of his dirty mind—accused Smitty of lying about the storm, maintaining that Smitty had really spent all that time chasing squaws. The flash of anger that appeared in Smitty's eyes puzzled Bob, who just happened to be watching him at the time.

Smitty had arrived home too late Sunday night to take Bob Bine his share of the elk. During all breaks, and the entire lunch period Monday, Bob and his coworkers pumped him about the trip. After work some of them even escorted him into the parking lot to view his trophy and help him transfer the remaining half of Harold's carcass into Bob's truck. All were envious of Harold's trophy head with its huge rack of antlers, the sight of which was beginning to sicken Smitty; nonetheless, a couple days later, he took it to a local taxidermist for mounting.

By the second day of his return, his fellow workers had lost all interest in Smitty's adventures, which suited him just fine. Thereafter, between each break period, the endless conveyer resumed its inexorable march onward, bearing a seemingly unending supply of split hog carcasses, from which he would deftly slash loins with his two-handed knife. The task required no brains, just muscles. More often than not, Smitty would switch his thoughts back to the pleasant memories of his tryst with LaVonne, which made the day pass more swiftly.

While pleasant memories made his work tolerable, evenings and weekends in his two-room walkup apartment were quite the opposite. Smitty was obliged to listen to innumerable calls from both his and Barbara's lawyers concerning the divorce settlement, child-care, and lawyer fees. The condition of his finances was none too good, and he was forced to spend considerable time calculating what he must do without in order to make ends meet. The little entertainment he could eke out came from an old black-and-white television that produced snowy pictures of bland offerings by the only two stations that its rabbit-ear antenna could receive.

Cable TV was out of the question because of the expense. He did, however, attempt to read history books borrowed from the public library, but with little success; he just wasn't able to concentrate on them for more than an hour at a time.

Across town, in Smitty's former home, on which he was still making payments, the cable television had become the sole property of his two daughters, who watched it unsupervised and at will. Barbara, who was yet Smitty's spouse, spent much of her time adorning herself for Paul Worthington, her new paramour. Barbara had become thoroughly enamored of the money and power Worthington controlled, and allowed the girls a free hand on the controls of the television. The only time their viewing was censored was when Barbara was out with Worthington, and her mother came over to supervise the girls.

The fact that Worthington had found a new lover soon became apparent to his wife, Paula, when she noticed that his usual selfish demands while in bed had again ceased. It was not the first time in their marriage this had happened; this time, however, she was ready to take action. She hired a private detective to begin recording Paul's actions, and the best divorce lawyer in the state to guide her own. Paula Worthington was convinced that Paul had hit his peak financially, and she was now ready to collect for fifteen years of a miserable and childless marriage.

Naïve, Smitty suspected nothing until one weekend when he was over visiting his daughters. Barbara, after taking a private phone call, asked Smitty if he'd mind watching the girls so she could go out shopping with her friend Mildred. Her mother was supposed to come at four-thirty and would take over then.

Smitty replied, "No problem. I was planning to treat them to hamburgers and a movie anyway."

"Take the car. I'll ride with Mildred," his estranged wife offered in a burst of generosity.

Returning to the house at four, Smitty was greeted by a phone call from his father-in-law, saying that Barbara's mom had become ill and that he was taking her to the hospital emergency room. At half past midnight, with the girls in bed sleeping, Smitty, asleep on the sofa, was awakened by the sound of a car pulling away from the curb. Shortly thereafter, a disheveled and intoxicated Barbara let herself in the front door.

"Good God, are you ever a mess! Don't try to tell me you've been out with Mildred. Frankly, I don't give a shit where you were! Your dad called and said he'd taken your mom to the hospital. She's okay and at home now. If I were you, I wouldn't try calling her at this hour in your condition. The kids are in bed, sleeping, and you're too damned drunk to be responsible for them. I'll stay here on the couch tonight. Get the hell up to bed! Go on. Don't worry, I wouldn't touch you on a freaking bet! You're disgusting! Why in hell don't we just hurry up and get this damned divorce over with?"

Three days later happened to be Thanksgiving This year, Smitty was not invited to dinner at Barbara's mother's as he usually was. Instead, he placed a phone call to LaVonne in Pierre.

"Get together to celebrate Thanksgiving? You've got to be kidding, Smitty. I suppose you expect me to bring a turkey and some pumpkin pies," she chided. "You expect me to give thanks that you *washiska* stole a whole continent from us?"

Silence.

"Okay, I was just kidding. I do have four days off, and I really would like to see you again. What would you like to do?"

"Could you meet me in Sioux Falls for the weekend?"

"I suppose. Could you afford the motel bill?"

"Not really."

"I suspected that. Why don't you come clear on out here to Pierre? My motel is cheaper, and you're welcome so long as you don't try to steal the towels," LaVonne said. "Actually, Tom and his wife have invited me to their place on Friday. I'm sure they

126

wouldn't mind if you came along. My mother will broil some elk over buffalo chips just for you."

"Ugh!"

"'Ugh'? When did you learn to speak Injun, Smitty," she teased.

"Damn, I miss you. Can I really come out?"

"Ugh, Ugh."

"Look, LaVonne, if you don't cut that out I won't bring you any beads!"

Because of the continued cold weather and the general unreliability of his old truck, Smitty, against his better judgment, used his credit card to rent a car for the holiday. Leaving immediately after work, he arrived at LaVonne's door shortly before midnight, clutching a suitcase in one hand and a string of beads in the other.

"How, Doe Eyes. Me got 'um pretty beads to trade for—"

"You just shut up and get in here before the neighbors hear you behaving like a fool," laughed LaVonne.

Again Smitty and LaVonne spent a delightful time together. He thoroughly enjoyed the family dinner with LaVonne's relatives. The dinner consisted of both turkey and elk. The turkey was excellent. The elk—old Harold—was just, well, tolerable, despite the efforts of all three women. "Ma" even managed to restrain herself somewhat and was civil toward Smitty.

On their third and final day, Smitty got up enough nerve to suggest that perhaps, once his divorce became final, and if LaVonne might consent, they ought to get married. Her reply only confused him more.

LaVonne said she would never move to Minnesota, as she believed she'd never be accepted there. Here in Pierre she felt she had been accepted, and proved it by pointing out the casual and friendly relationship she had with her boss Bill Verstegn. Also, she pointed out that Smitty probably would be paying child support for a good many years. Should he decide to try moving to Pierre, prevailing wages in South Dakota would hardly be enough for him to meet his obligations. Unless things somehow became different, she didn't see much chance it could happen. "Maybe someday, Smitty, we'll both get to a place where the grass is always green and the water runs forever."

"What do you mean by that?" he inquired.

"In years gone by, whenever whites and Indians signed treaties of peace, they always ended the treaty with, 'May this treaty last as long as grass grows green and water runs.' Beautiful thought, wasn't it? Sounds like a sort of never-never land, doesn't it?"

Smitty and LaVonne again parted on a rather sad note. Smitty hadn't received either a yes or a no to his proposal. But then, he hadn't really proposed.

Once again Smitty drove eastward across the cold and dreary prairie toward his lonely apartment and miserable job, feeling horribly alone, cold, and most depressed.

The Greek myth of Pandora, as it is commonly related, claims that after Pandora opened her box and released all the evils that plague mankind, one thing remained timidly hiding within—Hope! For most of his life, Smitty had clung tightly to hope—even more so now.

CHAPTER 23

The October blizzard that had caught Smitty at Pierre and happily confined him with LaVonne also caught up with Charles at the stockyards in Omaha, Nebraska, early Friday morning.

Prior to that, Charles had been confined in a small pen at the village of Eagle's stockyard until Wednesday afternoon, at which time enough other cattle of the necessary type had been purchased to make up a full load for transportation. Then he and two old bulls, who were both worn out and sterile, plus twenty-eight old and barren cows, were driven up a narrow chute leading into the trailer of the semi that would haul them to Omaha. They were all packed so tightly into the trailer that they would have to remain standing in the same position for the thirteen-hour ride.

Once there, Charles was herded into a small confining stall where he was held alone to prevent his fighting with other bulls.

Of all the cows who'd accompanied Charles from Colorado, those who were in reasonable flesh were immediately sent to a packing plant where they were slaughtered the same day. Their carcasses were hung in a huge cooler until Monday, when they'd be boned out and ground into hamburger for the fast-food chains.

It was there, in his small, exposed pen in the stockyard, that the blizzard caught up to Charles. He'd been fed nothing and watered but once since leaving Colorado. Throughout the blizzard of Friday and Saturday, the help at the Omaha yard valued their own comfort far more than that of the cattle in their charge, and neglected both feed and water. On Sunday, Charles received water; Monday, water again plus a little hay.

By the following Wednesday, enough old and decrepit range bulls had been assembled to fill out a truckload for shipment to a feedlot in Southern Minnesota, where they'd been consigned.

Thursday, Charles and twenty-nine other bulls were again driven up a chute and packed into the semi's trailer. All were jammed in so tightly that there was no possibility of their fighting, though Charles did manage to gouge the eye of an unfortunate polled Hereford bull who was jammed in next to him.

Approximately 400 miles and ten hours later, Charles and his fellow passengers were off-loaded at a feedlot, where they were supposed to fatten up enough to become quality bologna. Fattening bologna bulls is a business quite different from any other feeding operation.

For the first few days that any new group spent in the lot, a tranquilizer was added to their feed to prevent the bulls from fighting. All the pens in which they were confined were made of heavy, four-inch-diameter welded steel pipe, the confines of which no farmer in his right mind would ever enter while bulls were there. To further insure that the bulls would not fight, there could be no other farm nearby having female cattle. The scent of females in estrus would drive the entire batch of bulls quite mad.

One might ask why anyone would bother with all this effort and expense. Because of their coarse, stringy flesh, which absorbs water like a blotter, Bologna bulls command the same price as that of fancy fat steers. Often thin and rundown when purchased, bologna bulls can be bought cheaper than steers, and they put on weight much faster and more economically than steers fed the same amount. Feeding bologna bulls, though dangerous, is profitable.

Charles didn't acclimate well to the fattening rations. He actually preferred eating the straw bedding to the ground corn balanced with proteins and minerals offered in the feed bunk. He ate only enough of the prepared feed to supplement the nutritional deficiencies of the straw.

The tall iron-pipe fences almost completely thwarted his attempts to leap over them. On one occasion, however, he jumped up into the feed bunk and from there managed to leap over the fence to temporary freedom. His one and only escape lasted five days while the farmer and his hired help chased him all around the unfenced crop-farming countryside. Since there was no place to corner him, a veterinarian armed with a tranquilizer gun finally had to dart and immobilize Charles before he could be returned to his prison.

Ever afterward, and much to the consternation of the farmer, Charles continued to stand in the feed bunk simply to avoid the pushing and shoving of his cell mates. There was no chance for another dash to freedom, as the farmer had elevated the fence behind the bunk to prevent further escapes. Often, while standing in the bunk full of feed, Charles, like the elk and mule deer he'd associated with back in Colorado, would urinate onto the feed, which caused the other cattle to refuse to eat it—something the farmer didn't catch on to for two months.

Thereafter, when caught standing placidly in the feed bunk by the exasperated farmer, Charles was roundly cursed and prodded with a pitchfork, temporarily driving him from the bunk. Come March, the farmer gave up on fattening out Charles's frame and shipped him off to the packing plant.

CHAPTER 24

Ironically, the same judge granted both Smitty and Paul Worthington their freedom at roughly the same time, between Christmas and New Year's Day, and at considerable cost to each. The differences in their economic and social standings accounted for the short period of time that Paul and Paula Worthington had to wait for a court appearance, compared to the ten months Smitty and Barbara were required to wait. Swift "justice," if we may call it such, seems only for the wealthy, who appear to suffer the least from its administration.

The judge required Smitty, who had no savings and little equity, to continue making payments on the house and to make monthly child support and alimony payments until the house was paid off and the children reached adulthood. The alimony would stop only if Barbara remarried. Smitty left the courthouse financially burdened and mentally depressed.

His boss, on the other hand, left there smugly believing he'd struck a good deal. Paula was to get clear title to the house, most of the savings, and a cash settlement worth $2.2 million. In return she had to agree to forgo any claims against his future earnings. Despite having had to float a loan to arrive at the settlement, Paul Worthington was confident that he could manipulate the company well enough to recoup all of his losses and still gain much, much more within a very short time.

Smitty was required not only to pay his own lawyer, but to pay for Barbara's as well. Worthington paid only for his own counselor. Paula's lawyer, who worked on a contingency basis, received slightly over one third of the settlement. As is always the case, all of the advocates were very well compensated for their efforts.

The judge spent just minutes rendering his Solomonic decree on Smitty; whereas, three days later, during the Worthington trial, he retired to his chambers, supposedly to ponder the wisdom of his decision for a couple of hours. (He ate a sandwich, took a nap, and then rendered unto both sides exactly what they desired).

Adultery was a fait accompli in both cases, though Smitty, while suspecting his wife's behavior and knowing of his own, did not bring the matter up—nor would he have, even had he not been guilty. As a matter of fact, Smitty didn't even suspect who had cuckolded him until after the Worthington divorce, nor would he have ever known except for the fact that the editor of the local paper happened to be off on a Caribbean cruse, leaving an assistant in charge. The assistant, unlike the editor, had always been sympathetic to the union workers during the late strike, and published an article that cost him his job. Upon returning from vacation, the editor discovered, to his horror, that his assistant had exposed the paper to a possible defamation of character lawsuit, even though he knew Paul Worthington had absolutely no character at all.

The private detective Paula Worthington had employed had done his job well. A good many damaging photos of Barbara Smith and Paul Worthington had been taken, documenting them in many compromising situations, one of which happened to be of the pair boarding the company's corporate jet for a weekend tryst in Bermuda. Paula's lawyer introduced the photos hoping for sympathy from the judge, who was known to be an old fuddy-duddy.

The clerk of court—the daughter of a longtime packing-plant worker who refused to go back to work after the strike—just happened to "inadvertently" drop that particular photograph onto the floor in front of a reporter. The photo was reproduced in the paper, plainly showing the company jet, with the company logo on its rear end, and Paul Worthington's hand on Barbara's behind as they climbed aboard. The published picture and its accompanying story truly hurt Smitty, but, oddly enough, of all those who'd seen it, the only one who ever mentioned it to him was Bob Bine, who, upon seeing the hurt on his friend's face the following day, simply said, "Smitty, I saw it. I'm sorry."

Even nasty old Koehler managed to hold his tongue about the matter. The workers — all of them — came to hate Worthington even more vehemently than before. They all felt that he not only had screwed around with their livelihoods, but was also capable of doing the same with their wives.

From that point on, Smitty became so depressed that, for several weeks, he avoided his weekly visits with his daughters, drank heavily, and no longer bothered to call LaVonne. Once released from work, he would stop at a liquor store, purchase a twelve-pack of beer, go back to his miserable flat, and proceed to get drunk. Smitty's sorrow simply would not go away, nor would his sad-eyed constant companion.

Smitty had hung the stuffed head of Harold the great elk on the kitchen wall. The taxidermist had somehow managed to position the glass eyes in such a manner that they gazed balefully out into space, almost as if they too were about to shed tears of sorrow. Smitty, in his alcoholic stupor, often blamed most of his troubles on Harold. His family problems seemed to have begun right after his first hunting trip. Besotted and angry, Smitty would sometimes hurl empty beer cans at Harold.

His dislike for the trophy finally became so great that one night he tore it from the wall, threw it into the back of his truck, drove out into the country, and pitched it into a ditch alongside a country road. Even then Harold came back to haunt him. A passerby spotted it sticking out of the snow and alerted the newspaper, which then published a picture and a story of an elk buried to his neck in snow during the last storm.

By the end of January, Smitty's depression had grown to the point where he truly believed his life had completely fallen apart. Not a soul could buck him up. At work, Bob and old Stokey tried to cheer him up, and even Koehler let up on him.

One evening, when Smitty stopped in at his neighborhood on-off-sale liquor store for his daily beer ration, his old nerd high school buddy, Teddy, just happened by and bought Smitty a few beers, hoping he might somehow manage to cheer him up a bit. For a change, Teddy felt sorry for Smitty.

A few weeks before, as was his usual habit, Teddy had treated himself to dinner at one of the town's finer eateries. As the maitre d' was escorting him to his table, they happened to pass one occupied by Paul Worthington and Smitty's then wife Barbara. In passing, Teddy mumbled a flustered, "Hi, Barb," and was greeted with a pleasant enough, "Oh, hello, Teddy."

Paul, who almost always snubbed Teddy in the halls of the administration building where they both worked, said nothing.

Later, Paul commented to Barb, "That Teddy's such a damned insignificant nerd that when he dies he'll have to spend eternity in purgatory. Neither the Lord nor the devil will notice his presence."

Unfortunately, Teddy's table had not been beyond the range of Paul's cruel comment, or Barb's snicker.

CHAPTER 25

Teddy Berge, historian turned bean counter, had throughout his life been hurt a good many times before. In his early school days, the non-athletic, myopic Teddy was all too eager to display his knowledge of books. Throughout grade school, while armed with the right answers, his constant waving of his hand in the air became a trait that his fellow students found not very endearing. Later, in high school, having been branded a "nerd," he learned to hide both his knowledge and feelings, in what was by that time a vain attempt to be accepted by the rest of the kids.

Teddy's bachelor's degree in history had to date been of little use to him. Armed with such a degree, one could teach, work as an archivist in a museum, or continue to study and attempt to write history, which, without proper Ivy League credentials, would no doubt remain unpublished. Teddy found that jobs in museums were so scarce as to be almost nonexistent. As for teaching history in the public school system, history had already been swallowed by the new, all-inclusive, politically correct subject called "Social Science."

If one were to compare the textbooks concerning the Civil War published for, say, Georgia, Texas, the Midwest, and the New England states, he would be surprised to find four separate versions of the war. New England textbooks claim the war was fought to abolish slavery. Books from the Midwest claim it was fought to preserve the Union. Georgia's books claim the war was for the preservation of states' rights. Texas? Well, their textbooks maintain that Texas cavalry troops played the crucial part in every battle won by the Confederacy. The whole truth is, of course, invisible in all four versions.

In college, Teddy wrote his thesis concerning Sherman's role in the Civil War and the Indian wars following. Teddy was well aware that Sherman had lived in the South and admired the Southern way of life, yet had fought to save the Union. When left alone in Georgia, Sherman went out of his way to avoid pitched battles. He marched his troops throughout Georgia mainly to destroy the resources the South needed to continue fighting. Ironically named for the Shawnee leader, Tecumseh, Sherman was never an enemy of any Indian willing to reason.

At the conclusion of the war, Sherman was placed in charge of the West and the taming of the Western Indian tribes. He did not believe in confining them to reservations, and once wrote to Grant, his superior officer, "This whole subject of maintenance of Indians who won't work and must be fed is one that should be solved in Washington. I think we would better send them all to the Fifth Avenue Hotel to board there at the cost of the United States." Sherman was also well aware that "Indian Agents" appointed by do-good congressmen from back East were busy enriching themselves by cheating both the government and the Indians.

During an 1867 conference with the Cheyenne, Oglala, and Brule, who were demanding arms and ammunition that Sherman had refused them, a reporter named Henry Stanley (the same Stanley who four years later rescued Dr. Livingston in Africa) admired Sherman for having said to the tribes, "Look around you, the white men are taking all the good land for themselves. If you don't choose your homes now it will be too late next year. You cannot stop the building of railroads any more than you can stop the sun or moon. Our people East hardly think of what you call war out here, but if they make up their minds to fight they will come out as thick as herds of buffalo, and if you continue fighting you will all be killed. We offer you this, choose your homes and live like white men and we will help you. We are doing more for you than we do for the white men who come from across the sea."

"Well," wrote Teddy at the conclusion of his thesis, "such are the ways of treaties. Honored by few, ignored by more than many. No doubt there were a few 'noble savages,' but I suspect there were even fewer 'noble' white men. Damned few on either side rank alongside Sherman."

While working as an accountant at the plant, much of Teddy's spare time was spent in the local library, which happened to be a very good one. It had been endowed by the plant's founder, and had been jealously guarded over the years by his daughter-in-law, who in her old age lived for her library. It was there that Teddy was able to continue his study of the various tribes that either migrated or were pushed to the borders of the Great Plains.

He found that most of the seven Siouan-speaking tribes had been pushed there in the late seventeenth century. Some had timidly ventured there as early as the fourteenth century, but failed to thrive due to their lack of horses. Those early migrants eked out a meager existence by wandering great distances, packing all of their belongings on their backs and on the backs of their dogs. All the earliest settlers were more or less agriculturally oriented, and because the Great Plains were drought prone, they were forced to remain east of the Missouri River. Ultimately, when horses were procured from the Spanish and introduced onto the plains by the Caddoan-speaking Pawnee in the late eighteenth century, a whole new era dawned.

The Siouan-speaking tribes, thanks to their introduction to firearms and other trade goods by the French fur traders, came to dominate the northern portion of the Great Plains. The "Native American Sioux" owed much of their success to the Caucasians who arrived from Europe. For instance, the name "Sioux" was given to them by the French, who couldn't pronounce the Ojibwas' derogatory *nadoueissiw,* meaning "snake." The Sioux (snakes) referred to themselves as Lakota. The French fur traders, thanks to Europe's insatiable desire for head wear felted from beaver pelts, profitably plied their trade westward from the Great Lakes and northward up the Mississippi and Missouri rivers. Great Plains natives shortly became addicted to steel knives, hatchets, firearms, firewater, woolen blankets rather than fur robes, and—horrors—cotton canvas teepee coverings rather than cured buffalo hides; all of this, mind you, within the one hundred years or so that the Sioux dominated the Dakotas.

Brule, Miniconjou, and Sans Arc are names of three of the seven Siouan-speaking tribes of the Teton nation who had migrated onto the High Plains in the late seventeenth and early eighteenth centuries. Many Sioux names have French connotations. Teton is a derivative of the French word for breast: the Black Hills of South Dakota stuck up from the high plains much like a woman's breasts.

Quite unlike the inebriated Smitty, who never found out just who Pierre, South Dakota was named for, Teddy discovered that the buried lead plaque found on the east bank of the Missouri had been placed there by a son of Pierre La Vérendrye, who also had been named Pierre. Apparently, this son had been returning from an expedition to the Black Hills in 1738. That particular summer, the elder La Vérendrye remained in what is now south central Canada, traveling back and fourth between several of the fur-trading posts he'd established throughout southern Manitoba and Saskatchewan. Pierre, South Dakota, had in fact been named after Pierre Chouteau, a fur trader who'd ventured up the Missouri from St. Louis several years after Lewis and Clark's expedition.

French and French Canadians tended to get along better with the American Natives than did the English. The British colonists liked to talk down to their "Indians," telling them they were children of their "Great White Father" across the sea. The French, on the other hand, sent out *coureurs de bois* (young men) to live and trade with the natives. *Coureurs de bois* were both young and poor. They had a craving for two things the natives possessed: furs and nubile women, and were issued trade goods with which they could purchase both. Native males of the various tribes inhabiting mid-America so often fought with and killed each other that women outnumbered men two to one. Male-dominated Sioux were almost totally lacking in chivalry toward the feminine sex. A male, having failed to achieve orgasm during sexual intercourse, would often expectorate in the face of his companion for his failure. Hundreds of years before, gallant Frenchmen had discovered far more polite ways to achieve their desires.

Not all *coureurs de bois* were all that well versed in manners. In 1610, Champlain sent out young Etienne Brule to live with the Huron. Brule married into the tribe, and prospered so well that he became both wealthy and arrogant. He quarreled with his adopted people, who solved their problems with him by killing and eating him. All that remained was his name, which turned up on several rivers in the upper Midwest and, some two hundred years later, as the name of the Brule tribe of the "Teton" Sioux living along the Missouri River in territory once occupied by the Mandan Sioux.

Lewis and Clark's journals, read by Teddy Berge, mentioned having first met the Sioux near the mouth of the White River during the summer of 1804. Lewis referred to them as "The vilest miscreants of the savage race who will remain the pirates of the Missouri until our government makes them dependent on its will."

A bit farther up the Missouri, in the area around present-day Pierre, they came across the Arikara, a semi-agricultural tribe that spoke the Caddoan tongue and had migrated up from Oklahoma. Arikara were disliked by, and often at war with, both the Brule

Sioux on their south and the Mandan Sioux to their north. John J. Audubon, in 1843, found the Arikara most disgusting, partly because of their habit of munching on head lice plucked from each other, and partly because of the way they would retrieve a bloated rotten buffalo carcass from the river, then eat it with a spoon. Generally speaking, whenever an Arikara showed up, most everyone else moved on.

It was with the Mandan that Lewis and Clark wintered on their first year out. While there, they had the great good fortune to meet two French fur traders: Rene Jessaume and Toussaint Charbonneau. Charbonneau and his third wife, Sacagawea, whom he'd won from a Mintari brave by throwing dice, were hired to guide the expedition through Shoshonean territory farther west near the Rocky Mountains. The Shoshonean language was quite different from the Siouan dialects spoken by the Mandan and Teton Sioux.

The fact that Sacagawea was a Shoshone, and a sister to a Shoshone chief, and that she had been captured by the Mintari, probably saved the expedition from torture and death. The power-ful Shoshone were related to the dreaded Comache of the South. Both tribes tortured adult male captives to death. Shoshone and Comache would first cut both eyelids from their captives, so they could not avoid watching as the "noble savages" of the plains pro-ceeded to cut off other body parts such as fingers and genitals, etc. Ultimately, the victims were disemboweled and roasted over a slow fire. Disembowelment doesn't kill right away, and being roasted alive is the most painful death possible. (Wealthy people sentenced to die at the stake by their Roman Catholic inquisitors would often bribe their executioners to use green fagots, which would create enough noxious smoke that they, the victims, might more quickly and less painfully die from asphyxiation.)

The Sioux could be quite as cruel as the Shoshone. As late as 1855 a fur trader named Hercule Levasseru working out of Ft.

Pierre was captured by a tribe of the Teton Sioux and had both of his hands chopped off and his tongue cut out with the axes and knives that he was trying to trade for furs. Whenever the screaming of their tortured captives bothered their sleep, Sioux women would get up and go outside to cut out their tongues. This would effectively stop the noise.

Teddy Berge, the history nut, had also discovered that his Viking ancestors had also behaved with great cruelty. They would often slit between the ribs of a captive's back, reach in and pull his lungs out, and then laugh at the pretty butterfly staggering about in front of them.

The knowledge Teddy had gained served him to little avail. To date he had found no one with whom he could share his burning passion for history. Smitty and Teddy had come to share something in common: both had become somewhat isolated from society. Smitty's problems and Teddy's pursuit of history were of no concern to most of the town's self-centered general public.

CHAPTER 26

While Smitty may have felt that his life was falling apart, Paul Worthington's life was about to collapse about him.

When Paula's divorce papers forced him out of his house, Paul, having no place to stay, stayed several nights with Barbara and even slept in Smitty's bed, which pleased him greatly. Shortly thereafter he had all his things moved from his former home into a new, high-priced apartment found for him by a grateful Realtor. The place had been empty for six months since its construction, because it was too luxurious and was overpriced for the area. Barbara would have moved in also had she been asked. She wasn't asked. Rather, she was often called to appear upon demand.

Other than proposing that the company be split into non-union kill and union cut departments, Worthington almost disappeared from the local business scene. On a trip to Texas he contacted a rather shady Mexican fellow who was to set up a recruitment organization for the importation of cheap immigrant labor once the company was legally split.

Rather than attend to the day-to-day operation of the plant, he began to haunt high financial circles, ostentatiously leaving the impression that he was looking for other businesses that his company might take over—in either friendly or hostile manner. At the same time, in his travels, he sometimes left carefully disguised hints that he just might be willing to participate in a takeover (friendly or hostile) of the company that he now absolutely and ruthlessly ruled. The crew of the company jet saw many nights away from their homes and families due to Worthington's conniving.

Like a Roman emperor of old, Worthington now considered himself the master of his destiny and those of many others, and therefore felt no need to deny himself any personal pleasure. He was willing to cater to whatever senses gave him any pleasure, especially those involving power or sex, both of which gave him the same elevated sense of exhilaration. Throughout the months of March and April he traveled widely, while dallying with as many as two whores at a time. Back home he made do with Barbara.

Toward the end of April, Worthington began to feel weak and rundown. A visit to the local doctor sent him on to a university specialist whose diagnosis astounded Paul.

"I am quite sure you have developed a rather new ailment called AIDS, an acronym that stands for Acquired Immune Deficiency Syndrome. Your body is no longer capable of fighting disease. You've been infected with HIV, a virus that has just recently been discovered to exist. This virus seems to be transmitted through the body fluids, and is, more often than not, transmitted sexually. It's most commonly found amongst homosexuals. So far, at least, there is no cure—it's inevitably fatal."

As a person who had been capable of emotionlessly destroying others, Worthington, faced for the first time with the possibility that he himself might be the one destroyed, broke down completely in shock and tears. When Paul finally regained a bit of composure (he would never regain it completely), the physician asked, "Are you married?"

"I've been divorced for about four months," was the weak reply.

"Have you been with anyone else within the past year?"
"Several."

Raising his eyebrows somewhat, the physician asked, "Could you give me their names and how I might be able to notify them of the risk they face?"

"Just one. The others were only prostitutes; I don't even remember their names."

"Were any of them males?"

Weakly, "No."

"Well, you're a carrier now. You can be sure that if you remain promiscuous, you'll infect others. You wouldn't want to do that now, would you?"

Very weakly, "No.

"Well, I'll have my secretary make another appointment for you in about two weeks. As I said, we can only treat symptoms. I know of no cure. Perhaps someday, someone will find a cure. The disease, if it is a disease, progresses differently in different people. Some survive longer than others, but so far as I know it's always fatal."

Worthington received neither hope nor sympathy from this thirty-eight-year-old pragmatic virologist, whom he didn't like and who didn't like him either. Worthington much preferred sycophants. The young doctor was anything but.

When notified of her risk, Paula was both furious and frightened. Fortunately for her, in her desire never to have children by Paul, she had always insisted on his using a contraceptive. Paula escaped infection. She was fortunate. Barbara Smith was not.

CHAPTER 27

Upon his return from the university medical center, where many of his junior executives knew he'd been, all became aware of a drastic change in Paul Worthington. He no longer had any desire to travel about the countryside seeking more firms to devour, and more, and more varied, sexual pleasures. Instead, he arrived at his office in the plant late, left early, and behaved listlessly while there. Some felt he'd perhaps had a stroke, and informed J. B. Dalton, the chairman of the board. It was quite obvious to all that Paul was ill.

An emergency meeting of the board of directors was called, at which Worthington claimed to be a victim of cancer. The board checked his medical records and discovered the truth. Worthington was granted medical leave. Rather than allowing the company to suffer the indignity of having its CEO known to have contracted that new "queer" disease, Dalton leaked the information that Worthington had developed leukemia to the appropriate places.

When Barbara Smith discovered that she too was infected with the HIV virus, she immediately called Worthington. Paul tried to avoid her at first, but shortly discovered that she seemed to be the only person in the world with whom he had anything in common. Everyone else sought to avoid him, his true condition having become common knowledge, thanks to the wagging tongues of all those he'd trampled upon while climbing to the top of the dung heap.

Barbara eventually achieved her interview with Worthington, only to discover that he was even more frightened and confused than she. Upon consideration of her children's future, she consulted her mother, who, after her initial shock, sought to bring Smitty back into the picture.

Martha had never been very fond of her son-in-law. She blamed Smitty for having gotten her daughter pregnant and thus forcing an early marriage, but, in view of recent events, she had begun to suspect that not all that had happened was entirely Smitty's fault. Rather than trying to reach him by phone—she was too proud to attempt that—she talked to her next-door neighbor, a Mrs. Berge, whose son was still a bachelor and still living at home. Teddy, she knew, was a friend of both Barb and Smitty. Martha openly explained the problem to Teddy, who then tracked Smitty down and relayed both a peace feeler and the problem to him.

It was fortunate for all concerned that Teddy was called in as a mediator. Had Martha known of Smitty's drinking problem, she never would have tried approaching him. Teddy managed to catch up with Smitty before he'd begun his usual evening binge. The following day, shortly after work, Smitty, now sober and spruced up a bit, rang Martha's doorbell.

"Oh, hello, Smitty. I'm glad to see you decided to come," said Martha as she closed the door behind them.

"It's nice seeing you again too, but not under these conditions. Teddy told me about Barb."

"Well, come on into the kitchen. I'm baking. I'll make some fresh coffee. I guess you might remember that I feel more comfortable in 'my office.'"

The situation that Martha laid out ran thus: Barbara was quite sure that her AIDS would prove fatal. She did not want to expose her daughters to it, though her doctor had said that, with certain precautions, it wasn't contagious. Barbara wanted Smitty to move back into the house and take care of the girls with Martha's help, while she and Worthington would go out to California seeking help at a medical center that had a new experimental treatment for the disease.

The deal was cut, dried, and orally agreed to over Martha's kitchen table. After twelve years, Martha had finally made peace with Smitty. One might go even a bit further and say that, from that moment on, a bond had been forged between them.

When presented with these new facts, the same judge who'd granted Barbara her divorce granted custody of the children to Smitty and allowed him to move back into his home to finish raising his two daughters with the help of his mother-in-law.

Misery truly loves company, and, for the first time in his life, Paul Worthington discovered that he both wanted and needed companionship. Barbara moved in with him after she had arranged for her children's affairs. Once there, she was surprised to discover that Worthington was no longer obsessed with either power or sex. His prime concern now was his impending death and how he might avoid it. Barbara would become a combination of housekeeper, companion, and nurse — in short, a mother.

Soon thereafter, the two set off on a futile quest for a cure for the disease that now afflicted both of them. Before leaving, Worthington would perform the one, and probably only, good deed of his lifetime. Unbeknownst to the bank, from which he'd borrowed heavily, Paul, at the urging of Barbara, changed the beneficiaries of a mandatory very large life insurance policy, from the bank to Barbara's daughters. This good deed came not from the goodness within his heart. There was never any goodness there. He did it, first, because Barbara insisted — she had threatened to leave unless he complied. The second, and genuine, reason had come to him in an inspiration: he found pleasure in cheating the bank.

Meanness was a quality Paul would keep until his death. The consequence of his meanness was that Smitty's two daughters would each receive $500,000 when he died. In truth the gift came from their dying mother.

Neither Paul nor Barbara would survive long. Within two months, Worthington would expire in a California hospital, and with much plaintive bleating before lapsing into a final coma, just as had the mammoth thousands of years before in the Colorado quagmire. The body was cremated at Barbara's request. She returned to Paul's Minnesota apartment with the ashes. Once there she appeared before the same judge who had granted custody of the children to Smitty, where she, as Paul's common-law wife, claimed and was awarded his estate. The estate, which mainly consisted of stock options, was considerable. Barbara then wrote a will leaving all to her daughters, and named Smitty executor and Martha co-executor.

Having accomplished all that, Barbara performed one final act in secret: early one morning she drove to the waste-treatment plant and unceremoniously dumped Paul Worthington's ashes into a sewage aeration pond where they, appropriately, would be stirred along with the entire town's excrement. "It's done!" she sighed with satisfaction. "He gets what he gave."

Three weeks before Barbara's death, just after she entered the local nursing home, Smitty had tried visiting her. By that time, like the pliohippus who'd perished alongside the mammoth, she was becoming increasingly indifferent to the world and worldly things. One will never know whether she was contemplating what might have been, or what she might find on the other side of death's dark door.

CHAPTER 28

Throughout the winter that Smitty had lived alone in his miserable flat, he was fortunate to have been able to keep his old pickup truck in a garage shared with his landlord. The truck was a notoriously poor starter in cold weather. At work Smitty had taken to parking on the warmer, south side of the plant, beneath an exhaust fan that blew warm air onto the old heap. The south side just happened to be where the "beef kill" was located. Presently, the only beef killed were old bologna bulls, since fat, or prime, beef was no longer butchered at this plant. Some time ago, even before Worthington had assumed control, the company had purchased two smaller and more efficient plants located in Texas and Nebraska. Those not only were closer to the major beef feed lots, but also employed cheap, non-union migrant help imported from Mexico. The higher profit earned with cheap labor was a justification Worthington used later in his attempt to break the union. Almost all of the beef marketed by the company was slaughtered at those other plants. Bologna bulls, however, were still slaughtered and processed into "specialty meats" at the main plant.

In order to get from his truck to his job each morning, Smitty would pass by, and often stop to look at, the daily quota of bologna bulls awaiting slaughter in the pens. There were never more and seldom fewer than sixty bulls, all held under roof and tightly packed into small pens to keep them from fighting. More than once, as he passed by the condemned bulls, his thoughts returned to Charles the throwback, whom he'd twice driven down from the hidden mountainside pasture. At these times he often wished he'd never told Radson that he'd found Charles at the slide meadow.

From the holding pens, his route to work passed on through the area where the condemned would be killed, skinned, disemboweled, sawn in half, and then hung onto meat hooks dangling beneath the rail leading into a cooler.

That particular area of the plant had been allowed to run down. Wooden pens, chutes, and gates were becoming both old and rotten. The only reason Worthington hadn't closed the operation down was that most of the employees there would have to be transferred to other jobs within the plant because of union contracts concerning seniority. He would have much preferred laying them off and then replacing them with new help who would start at the minimum wage. As a matter of fact, before becoming ill, he'd instructed his staff to devise a plan whereby he could sell off any low-profit operations to a separate non-union company yet to be formed beneath and owned by the parent company. Paul's plan was still under study by the legal staff. The latest company president, an outsider just recently selected by the board—the first president who'd not been chosen from within the organization—would soon implement it.

Smitty, as he made his twice-daily trek through the beef-kill area, managed to become acquainted with both the help and their operation. Bulls were still killed by crowding them into a narrow chute; upon their reaching the end of it, they were stunned, one by one, with a sledgehammer blow to the head. One blow usually dropped them to the floor, where their throats were cut, and they would lie there kicking violently while bleeding to death. As soon as most of their convulsions ceased, two workers would pounce upon each carcass with sharp knives to skin out the legs and neck. Another worker would then saw off all four feet and the head. A hook was then shoved under the tendon of each hind leg, and a chain hoist would then snatch the carcass up. Other chains would then be attached to the hide, which then was winched off. The bull's carcass was then disemboweled, split in half, and trollyed off along the rail into the cooler, while the muscles of each half continued to twitch spasmodically.

One day in early March, while returning to his truck early after a short run, Smitty found the beef kill still hard at work. Their operation had been delayed because the ancient winch that powered all the chain hoists had broken down. Smitty also noticed that a plugged gutter was running over. Clotting blood and other assorted gore was almost ankle deep in the area. The dozen bulls remaining to be slaughtered had smelled the blood and were bellowing wildly.

God, a slaughterhouse is a horrible place! he thought. *Auschwitz or Dachau couldn't have been a hell of a lot worse than this. I feel like one of Heinrich Himmler's underlings!*

Just then a wiry little fellow standing on a platform alongside the chute, who had just neatly dispatched another bull with an effortless swing of his maul, said, "Hey Smitty. Did'ja get off early?"

"Hi, Pluto! Yeah, we had a short run," replied Smitty.

"Smitty, what's with this Pluto crap? Pluto is a dog in Disneyland. Why in hell do you keep callin' me Pluto? You know my name's Mal," said the little Irishman with the sledgehammer.

"If I explained it, you'd be pissed," grinned Smitty. "How's it going, Malcolm?"

"Ain't goin' worth a shit! Damned hoist broke down. Maintenance don't fix nothin' around this damned place. I think they're gonna shut this division down someday soon."

"I don't doubt it," returned Smitty. "Well, you take care now. Just watch out that you don't hit your foreman in the head instead of that next bull."

"Who the hell would care?" muttered Mal. "He's just as damned bullheaded as the rest of these damned fool bulls standing here in the chute."

"You got any idea how many bulls you've killed over the years?

"God, no! It's just a goddamned job. I don't even want to know. Don't try to make no goddamned philosopher out of me now. G'wan, get out of here. You go have a beer for me on your way home now. I still got to bop and stick another dozen of these worn-out old lovers before I c'n wet me whistle."

Smitty mused, *How could I explain to Mal about Pluto of Roman mythology? Pluto, the god of the underworld, would most kindly stun all of the not-so-good mortals with a mallet before feeding them to Orcus, the mythological monster of the underworld, who resembled a gigantic boar. How appropriate.*

"Mal, did you know that, with your mallet, you're feeding bologna to lots of ignorant people who democratically attempt to rule this old world?"

"Smitty, for crap's sake, stop playin' the bloody philosopher!" said Mal somewhat angrily. "You get the hell out of here before I bop you one on the head wit' me mallet here!"

All this happened within the time period when Smitty was still drinking for the express purpose of forgetting his problems. Smitty then proceeded to his truck while musing upon his college days and his ventures into Homer's *Odyssey,* where he'd read of Pluto, Orcus, and Hades. His truck, as usual, started fine, and, having been parked beneath the exhaust fan, smelt rather like ham and manure cooked in the same pot. The whole plant, at times the whole town, smelled that way; all the inhabitants of both had become so used to the stench that they didn't realize it existed.

Smitty then drove to the public library, borrowed a book on the Great Plains, and then went on to the liquor store for another twelve-pack. Since the plant employed most of the residents of the city, neighborhood liquor stores managed to gross enough to provide their owners a reasonable living. There were numerous neighborhood liquor stores in this town.

Upon arriving home, Smitty opened a bag of chips, a can of beer, and the book he had just checked out. Beginning to read, he was surprised to discover that Sioux and Mandan were related tribes, and that the Sioux, the most glorified tribe of the Great Plains, were not the first to venture onto them.

The Sioux, Mandan Sioux included, were agriculturists who migrated from present-day Minnesota. The Arikara, a tribe speaking the Caddoan tongue, had arrived from the south some one hundred years prior. As always, the cultures and mores of the newest arrivals replaced those of the first inhabitants, perhaps because of the original people's inability to converse with those new arrivals, who, in their own opinion, knew everything worth knowing.

The Sioux, as they evolved out on the plains, with its vast supply of buffalo, gave up agriculture and became hunters and gatherers, and shortly became the dominant tribal nation of the Great Plains.

The Mandan remained farmers, and, because they were the first plains tribe to come into contact with French fur traders, they shrewdly maneuvered themselves into an intermediate position between the French and other tribes.

By the time Smitty had finished one chapter he'd also finished his third beer, so he might not have remembered some of the aforementioned bits of history. Approximately half, he failed to retain due to self-induced alcoholic stupor. He might not have understood that, shortly after La Vérendrye's traders first made contact with the Mandan, disease wiped out three of their five villages, and that smallpox brought by traders following Lewis and Clark killed off all but thirty-one of those 1,500 still alive in 1837.

LaVonne DeLorme had a paternal grandmother some nine generations in the past, born of a young Mandan maid who'd become enamored of one of La Vérendrye's *coureurs de bois.* That fall, he bid her adieu to return to his wife and children in Montreal by saying, *"C'est selon"* ("That is as may be"). The statement proved quite accurate, for a year and a half later, she contracted measles and died, leaving a nine-month-old, blue-eyed boy to be raised by an aunt from the next village north. The boy survived, grew up, married, and had a daughter who, in 1805, fell in love with one of Lewis and Clark's French engagés who had accompanied them from St. Charles, Missouri. That particular engaging lad also left his young maiden pregnant and with the airy phrase, *"C'est selon,"* as he climbed aboard the keelboat returning to St. Charles the following spring. The little blue-eyed girl resulting from that alliance, and her mother, survived the smallpox epidemic of 1837 that occurred when the steamboat *St. Peter* brought the disease up the Missouri. Out of a population of 1,600 a mere thirty-one Mandan survived. Among the little girl's descendants, generations in the future, would be LaVonne DeLorme.

LaVonne's ancestors would interbreed with the French once more before she was born. Shortly after Lewis and Clark returned to St. Louis, one Pierre Chouteau from St. Louis built a trading post at Fort Pierre on the west side of the river. Both Fort Pierre and Pierre, which lay on the opposite side of the river, were named after him. One of his clerks working at the post took a Sioux bride, and through marriage, gave her and their children the Catholic faith and the surname DeLorme.

Had Smitty been made aware of the way LaVonne's ancestors were woven into the past, he might have become interested enough to have remained sober, but of course he could not, as this minuscule portion of history had never been recorded. It just happened.

C'est selon.

CHAPTER 29

L ife for Smitty was totally different now that he had been reunited with his daughters. Evenings were quite routine. The girls were allowed to watch television while the evening meal was being prepared. After dinner, Smitty helped them with their homework before Gramma Martha saw to it that they were bathed and off to bed by nine-thirty. Smitty and his mother-in-law viewed the ten o'clock news, following which Smitty was off to bed with his book.

Reading didn't always make him drowsy as it had in his drinking days. It hadn't then, either—the alcohol had. Despite his recent heavy drinking, Smitty hadn't become thoroughly addicted. Back when he'd been forced to live alone in his miserable flat, alcohol had helped him blank out all thoughts of what he craved but seemed to be denied by society: a loving wife, children, close friends, plus an occupation, not just a miserable dead-end job. He now had all but the wife and the decent job.

Alcohol was, and still is, a problem confounding many Native Americans. Tribal leaders signed away huge tracts of land for little more than a few drinks of rum or whiskey. The French and English proffered rum from their Caribbean islands, while the "Americans" offered whiskey, often laced with a bit of gunpowder or strychnine to enhance its effect. One might rather suspect that whites didn't zip up their own booze with such, even though absinthe (cognac laced with wormwood and laudanum) was quite popular in certain circles.

There is a physiological difference between Caucasians and Orientals, of whom Indians are descendants. The livers of Caucasians are capable of breaking alcohol down into simple sugars, whereas those of many Orientals are not. Alcohol consumed by Native Americans goes directly into the bloodstream and is conveyed to the brain in stupefying quantities.

Giving up his alcohol overindulgence had been no great problem for Smitty. He didn't need any counseling to realize that, if he should quit, he himself would have to will it. He felt it was like the process of learning. The best teacher in the world cannot force students to learn anything, for the student, by his own will, learns.

Before falling asleep, Smitty often thought of LaVonne and his dreary job at the plant. He decided that if he were to have one, he must give up the other. Now, thanks to Barbara's will and Paul Worthington's ill-gotten money, he was no longer bound to his miserable employment. He had, with his mother-in-law's blessing, arranged a meeting with LaVonne during Easter vacation, when he planned to tender another proposal of marriage. They were to meet in Sioux Falls, where he'd reserved motel rooms for all. He wanted LaVonne to meet his daughters, and hoped they might make a favorable impression. The girls were thrilled at the prospect of staying in a motel with a swimming pool. So was Grandma, who was to go along to mind the girls in order to allow Smitty and LaVonne some time together. All were looking forward to the meeting. LaVonne, however, had some misgivings, for, unknown to anyone other than her doctor, she was four months pregnant with Smitty's child.

Meanwhile, back in Minnesota, while rummaging through some of his old college textbooks just five days before the Smith family was due to leave for Sioux Falls, Smitty came across one from an elective class he'd taken. Entitled *Ancient Societies of Man,* the book had, tucked between its pages, some notes Smitty had made in years gone by. One read, "If one were to compile a list of all histories, one would discover that nearly all were written by men, not women; and history, as recorded by male historians of old, often placed the blame for all of the woes of Man onto Woman. The *Talmud* blamed Eve, the first woman, for causing man to live forever in a troubled world. Hundreds of years later, Greek mythology blamed Pandora for releasing all the woes afflicting mankind."

The following day Smitty stopped by the library and picked up an English translation of the Greek myths from Hesiod's version of Homer. One of the myths transcribed therein pertained to Pandora, a beautiful and capricious woman whom Zeus created from clay as a gift to the mortal Epimethus, who owned a box containing all the evil spites that could afflict mankind. Forbidden by her husband to open the box, Pandora nevertheless did so, and out flew all the evil spites but for one — Hope — who remained hiding therein. Alas, Hope too was a spite! The ancient meaning of the word "spite" was chagrin, disappointment, vexation; Hope, therefore, merely made deceitful promises.

As Smitty was soon to learn, one needs far more than the false promises of Hope to survive; one must strive to shape one's own destiny.

CHAPTER 30

Three days before his planned trip to Sioux Falls to see LaVonne, Smitty, as was his habit, parked his truck on the south side of the plant.

This time, however, as he trudged through the holding pens toward his work station, he noticed a familiar-looking small red bull with erect horns. Closer inspection revealed the "Ch" branded on his flank. Destiny had once more thrown Charles and Smitty together.

Mal, the little Irishman who killed all the bulls, happened to be following behind Smitty on their way to work, and overheard Smitty say with astonishment, "Oh, my God, its Charles!"

"What'n hell are you rantin' about, Smitty? Say, are you okay? You look like you're sick."

"Dammit! Just leave me alone. I'm all right. It's just the whole damned rest of this rotten world that's sick!"

"Touchy, touchy!" muttered Mal as he watched Smitty plod dejectedly off to his job in the hog cut.

As the morning progressed, all of Smitty's coworkers wondered what had come over him. He snapped angrily at whoever tried to speak with him. During the first two work breaks he morosely slouched off by himself. On the second break of the morning, Koehler asked of Smitty's buddy, Bob Bine, "What the hell's eating him?"

"Cripes! I don't know," observed Bob as he lit his cigarette.

159

"I'm almost afraid to ask."

Along about ten o'clock the hog cut began to buzz with a story that circulated up and down the line: "Did'ja hear about the accident over on the beef kill? Some damned wild bull broke out and gored a couple guys. Had to call the ambulance and haul 'em both off to the hospital! One's hurt real bad!" The story reached Smitty's area less than ten minutes after the event happened.

"Charles! Oh, my God! I'll bet it was Charles," exclaimed Smitty to no one in particular, whereupon he threw his knife onto the floor and just stood staring off into space.

"Smitty! What in hell are you doing?" shouted his foreman. "Get back to work! You're screwin' the line up!"

Smitty didn't say a thing. Instead, he rudely pushed past his foreman and stalked off toward the beef kill, which happened to be in the same direction as the first-aid station.

"Dammit!" screamed the foreman. "Hit the button. Shut the damn line down. You sick or something, Smitty? You'd damn well better be sick or I'll get you fired!" he shouted toward Smitty's receding figure. "Okay, guys, start the line up again. I'll try to take his place. I haven't pulled loins for years." The foreman was angry for having to physically work for the remainder of the day.

Once Smitty reached the beef-kill area he was shocked at what he saw. Charles was dead. His body lay tangled in the mechanism of the ancient hoist. Mal, the little Irishman, was strutting about, boasting, "That damned crazy bull busted out, knocked Sam down, and pinned Ed up agin' the wall. By God, I took care of 'im, didn' I, fellas?"

What had actually happened occurred when Charles was locked at the end of the chute to be stunned. As Mal started to swing his maul, Charles caught sight of the descending hammer, tossed his head, and took the smashing blow upon his nose rather than on his forehead, which failed to drop him. The pain so infuriated him that he began violently lunging about. Mal dropped the

160

maul and was then thrown from his platform, accidentally tripping the latch, which opened the side of the pen, thus freeing Charles. Now thoroughly enraged, Charles charged one of the hapless skinners who was running away in fright, and tossed him over the fence much like a bleeding rag doll.

Ed, the foreman, ran to his desk, pulled open a drawer, and yanked out a rusty .45 caliber automatic pistol that was kept there for just such emergencies. Due to neglect, its rusted condition caused the pistol to fire only one round, then jam.

Charles was only wounded in the neck. He charged at and caught Ed in the corner of the room, where he gored him repeatedly. By this time Mal had regained his composure enough to seize a fire ax from the wall and attack Charles from the rear. Whirling about to face his new adversary, Charles happened to catch sight of a bit of light streaming into the room from its only window, and, trying to escape his tormentor, ran toward it. Between Charles and the window sat the ancient winch with its unprotected whirling chains, belts, and gears. As he bolted toward the light and freedom, Charles became entangled in the revolving gears. There he was hacked to death by Mal with his fire ax.

Viewing the carnage shortly afterward, Smitty cried aloud, "Oh, my God! Why? He could have made it if we'd just left him alone. Goddamitall!" he cried, and then ran out the door, jumped into his truck, and, with little thought, drove onto the freeway, right in front of a large truck, which swerved to avoid a collision. The blast of the truck's air horn brought Smitty back to reality. He pulled off at a nearby truck stop where, after a contemplative cup of coffee, he called LaVonne at work.

"LaVonne, it's me, Smitty."

"Hi, Smitty. Is something the matter? Why are you calling me at work?

"Are you too busy to talk for a couple minutes?"

"No. I'm just sorting through the mail. Bill's off arguing a case to the state supreme court. What's the problem?"

"Ah, well, I guess there's no real problem. It's just that something happened this morning. I want to talk to someone about it. You're the only one who could understand."

"I don't know, maybe I might."

"Well, I never told you that I crossed paths with a crazy, wild sort of bull both of the times when I went hunting out in Colorado."

"Bull elk, like the one you shot?"

"Naw, a bull, a cow bull."

"What's that to get so upset about?" asked LaVonne.

"Aw, hell. The critter was just a calf when I first saw him."

"Have you been drinking, Smitty?"

"Oh, for cripes sake, no!" exclaimed Smitty, who then went on to explain how his life and that of Charles had become so entwined. After relating the final episode of his relationship with Charles the throwback, Smitty said, "God, I feel awful about it all. Maybe I could have done something. I don't know. But, I did learn something. Do you remember when you told me about how treaties between whites and Indians always contained the phrase 'So long as grass grows green and water always flows'?"

"Yes, I do, but what has that got to do with it?"

"Do you remember how I then told you about that 'Hope' thing who remained in Pandora's box?

"Mm, I guess I do."

"Well, would you believe it, just last night I was reading a book on Greek mythology and found out that Hope was also a spite, a bad person, and always made false promises saying that she would make everything better. Well, Hope is a liar. That darned little red bull named Charles just showed me that if one wants to have something better from life, he damned well better do something about it. LaVonne, I'm going to quit this damned stupid job. I'm going to move out to Pierre, and I'm going to propose marriage to you when we get together in Sioux Falls."

"Smitty!"

"LaVonne, I can't wait until we can get together."

After hanging up, Smitty went back to the plant's administration building and requested personal time off, and some of his unused vacation time, to straighten out his affairs. Actually, Smitty intended to use all of the aforementioned time to seek both a wife and another occupation. Thanks to Charles's effort to survive, Smitty had come to realize that Hope had absolutely nothing to offer.

If one hopes to alter his destiny he ought to at least, thought Smitty, *do something more than passively stumble down life's chute toward Pluto's mallet and then be devoured by a goddamned hog named Orcus.*

CHAPTER 31

About one o'clock of the day that Charles had been hacked to death, Teddy Berge, while returning to his cubicle from the lunchroom, happened upon Smitty waiting to be seen by the personnel director. By that time, Smitty had regained his composure enough to disguise his true feelings. (In the United States, those who earn their bread with their hands are not supposed to have feelings — especially slaughterhouse workers.)

"Hi, Smitty. What brings you over here amongst us pencil pushers?"

"Oh, hi there, Teddy. Didn't notice you coming down the hall. Guess I was just too wound up in my own affairs."

"Nothing wrong, I hope?"

"Nah, just lookin' for some time off. I want to go out West for a while."

"Where out West? I've never been more than fifty miles west of here."

"Oh, just out to Pierre," said Smitty, who then unexpectedly blurted, "I gotta get the hell out of this damned plant before I go nuts! I'm goin' out there to look for work."

"Hey, Smitty, it's almost quitting time for me. When you get done here let's get together for a brew. I'd like to get the hell out of here too."

At the local pub Smitty downed a coke, and Teddy one beer. Smitty spilled his guts to Teddy — and Teddy finally had found a friend.

Two days later, Smitty, daughters, and mother-in-law reached the Sioux Falls motel an hour before LaVonne. When LaVonne arrived, she was told at the desk that all were in the pool. It was an interesting meeting. Both LaVonne and Smitty were shy. His daughters, when introduced, behaved exactly as ten- and twelve-year-olds would be expected to. Martha was both reserved and curious.

"Hello, Smitty."

"LaVonne—" replied Smitty. "Oh, excuse me, I'd like you to meet my mother-in-law Martha. Martha, this is LaVonne."

"I'm pleased to meet you," both politely said.

"Those two kids splashing around in the pool are my daughters." It took a bit, but eventually all became comfortable with each other.

Martha's appraisal of LaVonne was favorable. Wise in the ways of women, Martha could sense that LaVonne was obviously pregnant, but was nonetheless drawn toward her. As the extended weekend progressed, Martha, when the opportunity arose, gave her blessing to Smitty's proposed proposal.

Smitty and LaVonne had their time together later in the motel's bar, where, after having his proposal interrupted by LaVonne's tearful confession that she was pregnant, he then pressed his case ever more ardently. LaVonne accepted.

Smitty had reserved two rooms with double beds. Martha and the girls occupied both beds in one of the rooms; in the other, one bed remained empty.

The three-day weekend passed in the twinkling of an eye. Smitty returned his children and mother-in-law to Minnesota, and immediately repacked his suitcase for another trip to South Dakota—this time to Pierre. Despite her Catholicism, LaVonne and Smitty were married in a civil ceremony. LaVonne's boss and his wife, the Verstegns, acted as witnesses.

Smitty's search for employment was not quite as successful.

Toward the end of his quest he came across the elderly owner of a tire shop, who just happened to be approaching retirement age. Smitty's request for a job was countered with an offer: With just a small down payment Smitty could have a minor partnership, with the possibility that he might ultimately purchase the whole business. The owner cited the fact that tires wore out long before cars did, while people, no matter how hard times became, were not about to stop driving, and Dakotans were forced to drive many miles, as anywhere in South Dakota was a hell of a ways from everywhere else. Smitty accepted with the astonished realization that he might someday become his own boss.

It took Smitty two months to dispose of his house and move out to Pierre. Oddly enough, Martha accompanied him. Recently, Martha's entire life had come to revolve about her only grand-daughters. She volunteered to move to South Dakota sight unseen in order to be with them. LaVonne, not wishing to give up her job, agreed to the arrangement. All moved into a large old house on State Street that Smitty had purchased with the equity he'd accumulated from the sale of his house back in Minnesota.

Three months later, upon the birth of his son, no one on earth could have been happier than Smitty.

As time wore on, Smitty's daughters completed high school and went on to a private college back in Minnesota. Both did well and both married well. Smitty and LaVonne's son grew up to be up to be a short, dark-haired, blue-eyed, handsome young fellow; he is presently off to college, seeking to graduate with an English major and a minor in history.

As of today, the end of this narrative, Smitty could count twenty satisfied years in Pierre, South Dakota.

EPILOGUE

A uthors quite often introduce themselves toward the end of their books in an epilogue, as I am now doing. As you may have suspected, I happen to be Theodore Berge, the inconspicuous nerd who surfaced occasionally throughout the story.

Why, you may ask, has it taken me so long to write and get published? First and foremost was the pursuit of my own life and career; secondly, I found it most difficult to write about Smitty during his lifetime. Finally, I must mention the difficulty of finding a publisher. In today's mercantile age, publishers seem interested only in best-selling authors or ghostwritten books concerning public celebrities.

After visiting with Smitty years ago when he abruptly decided to leave the plant, I too made up my mind to do something else. I've since evolved from a short, fat, balding twenty-seven-year-old accountant into my present state: a short, fat, completely bald curator of a historical museum. The summer that Smitty moved his family west, I bought myself a pickup truck with a camper and headed west on a vacation. I never returned, and have never been sorry for not having done so.

It is possible that, had I stayed on, I might have risen high in the accounting department. By gobbling up a good many other small corporations, the plant, following Paul Worthington's lead, went on to become a mega-corporation in the food industry. That it has done extremely well I can personally attest to, as my small amount of stock certainly flourished.

In my roamings throughout the West, I followed Lewis and Clark on their trek across the nation. I followed the trails of exploring mountain men and Mormon emigrants. I visited the site of Custer's ignominious last stand. I even went to Colorado and became acquainted with the Radsons. Would you believe it, while there I somehow managed to climb the bald-topped mountain and found the slide meadow all by myself. Unfortunately, I didn't manage to see any of the wild cattle that Radson was complaining about. It seemed that a type of small horned cattle had evolved that were plaguing the local ranchers. They were more elusive than wild elk and could jump fences like deer.

Several times, during my travels, I stopped by at Pierre to keep in touch with Smitty. I met LaVonne and her small son Loren. While there, Martha, my former neighbor from Minnesota, as always, lured me into her kitchen to sample her wares (alas, I love sweets!). LaVonne very kindly prevailed on some of her politician friends in the capitol to get me appointed as an assistant curator of their new historical museum, for which I shall be eternally grateful to her. Just recently I moved up to become the curator.

LaVonne, bless her, introduced me to another friend of hers: a nurse of Swedish ancestry from the local hospital. Blond, slender, almost a head taller than I, we somehow became man and wife. I could not be happier.

Even though we have no children of our own, we were privileged to watch and help Smitty's children achieve adulthood. We became "Aunt Eve" and "Uncle Ted" to all three of them, and, thank heavens, in my work I'm now known as Theodore Berge. I always detested the "Teddy" handle.

As is ever the case, life is always followed by death. Two winters ago, Smitty, out shoveling snow, succumbed to a massive heart attack. It was a sad occurrence in all our lives. As for Smitty, who knows? I expect not. It would seem better to depart from a happy life than from a sad one, and the last twenty years of Smitty's were certainly happy (as have been my past twenty years).

I have been told that memories are the only things one may take into the next world. If that is so, then both Smitty and I shall be bearing large portfolios of pleasant memories when we arrive at St. Peter's gate. How sad it would be if one had naught but sad memories to take to his next place of residence.

I have no idea just how the reading public shall receive this book. In this electronic age, the reading of books has become passé. Nonetheless, I've enjoyed both the writing of it and my part in it.

Life, as most everyone experiences it, is neither all happy nor all sad, nor is it simply a roller-coaster ride with moments of elation, fear, and depression. Thanks to the exemplary life of Charles, both Smitty and I finally attempted to direct our own affairs. Fate, some say, plays an equal part. I find that quite doubtful in the case of Paul Wentworth and Barbara Smith. Had they made other choices, they might have altered their final fate. In the case of Charles, who knows? Against all odds, he, at least, tried. Perhaps his life here on earth was a success. His offspring seem to be surviving on and about the bald Colorado mountain.

Perhaps LaVonne, standing at Smitty's gravesite, summed it up best when she said, *"C'est selon."* Then she wiped away a tear and repeated, *"C'est selon."*

Resources

While I understand that a bibliography is not needed for a novel, I shall offer a few of many books that may have influenced the writing of Charles the Throwback.

Furthermore, all the characters are fictional. I am neither Smitty nor Teddy.

Charbonneau, Louis. *Trail* (a novel).

Frazier, Ian. *Great Plains.*

Graves, Robert. *The Greek Myths* (complete edition), 1955.

Hyde, George E. *Red Cloud's Folk: A History of the Oglala Sioux Indians.*

Hyde, George E. *Spotted Tail's Folk: A History of the Brule Sioux.*

Lazarus, Edward. *Black Hills, White Justice.* HarperCollins.

Lewis, Lloyd. *Sherman* (biography).

Michener, James. *Texas* (a novel).

Milton, John R. *South Dakota (a history).*

Morrison, Samuel Elliot. *The Oxford History of the American People.* Oxford University Press.

Reader's Digest Assn., Inc. Pleasantville, NY. *The Story of America (America's Fascinating Indian Heritage).*

Utley, Robert M. *The Last Days of the Sioux Nation.* Yale University Press.

Wilkins Campbell, Marjorie. *The Northwest Company.* Macmillan (Toronto).

— *ted owen*